The Traitor
Within

www.**rbooks**.co.uk
www.**bbc**.co.uk/**merlin**

Also available:

For younger readers:

The Traitor Within

Text by Mike Tucker

Based on the story by Julian Jones

BANTAM BOOKS

MERLIN: THE TRAITOR WITHIN
A BANTAM BOOK 978 0 553 82221 2

First published in Great Britain by Bantam,
an imprint of Random House Children's Books
A Random House Group Company

This edition published 2010

1 3 5 7 9 10 8 6 4 2

The Random House Group Limited supports the Forest Stewardship Council
(FSC), the leading international forest certification organization. All our titles that
are printed on Greenpeace-approved FSC-certified paper carry the FSC logo. Our
paper procurement policy can be found at www.rbooks.co.uk/environment.

Mixed Sources
Product group from well-managed
forests and other controlled sources
www.fsc.org Cert no. TT-COC-2139
© 1996 Forest Stewardship Council

Typeset in 12/18 Bembo by Falcon Oast Graphic Art Ltd.

Bantam Books are published by Random House Children's Books,
61–63 Uxbridge Road, London W5 5SA

www.**kids**at**random**house.co.uk
www.**rbooks**.co.uk

Addresses for companies within The Random House Group Limited can
be found at: www.randomhouse.co.uk/offices.htm

THE RANDOM HOUSE GROUP Limited Reg. No. 954009

A CIP catalogue record for this book is available from the British Library.

Printed and bound in Great Britain by CPI Mackays, Chatham, ME5 8TD

*With grateful thanks to Johnny Capps,
Julian Murphy, Polly Buckle, Rachel Knight,
Sarah Dollard, Jamie Munro, Pindy O'Brien,
Filiz Tosun, Anna Nettle and Rebecca Morris*

Chapter One

The Great Dragon was free.

Even after the best part of a year, Merlin still found it difficult to believe. From his very first day in Camelot, the Dragon had been there, a constant presence in his mind, guiding him, helping him. Using him.

Merlin knew now that whatever advice and assistance the Dragon had provided, it had always been trying to win its freedom. The creature had been cunning, and Merlin had been the one who had loosened its bonds.

Camelot still bore the scars of the Dragon's attack – three nights when it had wreaked terrible vengeance against those who had killed its kind and bound it with chains. In the end the kingdom had only survived because of powerful magic, but that victory had come at a dreadful cost.

For Merlin that cost had been especially high. The death of his father, the Dragonlord, had been a terrible blow, and yet even the pain of that loss paled next to the act of betrayal that the Dragon had made him commit.

Morgana. The king's ward, Arthur's childhood companion, Gwen's mistress . . . Merlin's friend. Morgana, whose troubled dreams had been a foretaste of her own magic power beginning to emerge. She had been the only one save for Gaius who might have understood the loneliness that Merlin felt, with the burden of magic that sat upon his shoulders. And yet, if the Great Dragon was to be believed, she was evil, a witch who would stop at nothing to destroy the kingdom with her magic. Given the alliance that she had formed with the sorceress Morgause, it seemed the Dragon had been right.

And so Merlin had poisoned her. He could still see the look of pain and disbelief on her face as he had cradled her in his arms, waiting for the hemlock to do its work; could still hear the breath rasping in her throat as she struggled to draw breath. He knew that he had had no choice, that the fate of the entire kingdom had rested on that dreadful act, but still Merlin had the most dreadful feeling that all their lives had been changed for ever by the decision he had made.

In the end he had saved the kingdom. Morgause had called off her attack in return for the name of the poison that he had used, spiriting Morgana away to heal her, and releasing Camelot from the power of her spell.

The king knew nothing of Morgana's treachery, or of Merlin's part in stopping her. All he knew was that magic had threatened his kingdom and taken his ward from him, and his anger was terrifying.

From the moment the Dragon's attacks had ceased, he had sent men out to search the countryside. They never stopped, charged to search day and night until Morgana was found. Uther Pendragon was a hard man at the best of times, but the loss of his ward had made him vicious and obsessive, refusing to accept the slightest excuse, refusing to acknowledge that failure was even an option. And so the quest had gone on – weeks, months, a year . . .

The Knights of Camelot had lost so many of their number in the battle with the Dragon, and now, staring out across the desolate plain that stretched in front of him, Merlin realized that many more would lose their lives in service to Uther before this search was over.

Red cloaks, royal symbols of the court of Camelot, fluttered like flags amongst the bodies of the fallen soldiers, mercifully obscuring the blood that stained the ground. Merlin cast a look at Arthur, who rode alongside him, seeing grief and anger flash across the young prince's face. When Arthur spoke, it was with little hope.

'See if there are any survivors.'

Guilt at the sight of so many more dead twisted like a blade in Merlin's chest.

Uther stood at a window of the palace, staring out at the distant hills. It was the same every day, a silent vigil, interrupted by only the boldest of courtiers, and then only with the most pressing of court business.

Gaius watched silently, waiting for the king to acknowledge his presence. Finally Uther turned, his once proud face pale and haunted.

'Has Arthur made contact with the patrol?'

The court physician shook his head regretfully. Pain and disappointment flashed momentarily across the king's face and he turned back to the window.

'Sire . . .' Gaius kept his voice low and calm. 'How many more men are you going to lose in this quest?'

'As many as it takes,' said Uther coldly.

The old man steeled himself, aware that what he was about to say would not be welcome. 'I need to speak to you as a friend.'

Uther stiffened. 'I have no time for friends.'

Gaius was not going to be intimidated. He had known Uther a long time and was perhaps the only man in Camelot to whom the king might listen. 'Then I'll speak to you as your physician. This is madness. It has been a year now. When are you going to stop?'

Uther turned and fixed Gaius with a piercing stare that left him in no doubt that the king was resolute in the path that he had set himself and his people.

'When Morgana is found.'

Arthur crouched down, examining the hoof marks that had churned up the ground. 'Seems their attackers headed north,' he murmured.

He rose, swinging himself up expertly onto his horse. 'Come on.'

Merlin looked at the fallen bodies anxiously. 'You think we should be going after them?'

Arthur gave his servant a look of weary resignation. 'Merlin, you're such a girl's petticoat.'

The party rode north, the terrain changing from open plains to undulating hills and finally to twisted forest. Their pace slowed. The forest was thick and swathed in fingers of drifting mist, ideal territory for an ambush. Arthur looked round for Merlin. He had fallen behind again. Finally a horse emerged from the fog, Merlin bouncing around uncomfortably in the saddle.

'Is there something wrong with you?' chided the prince.

'I've been on a horse all day!' complained Merlin.

'Ah . . . Is your bottom a little sore?'

'Yeah. It's not as fat as yours.' Merlin urged his horse forward, pushing past his master.

Arthur followed him, amused. He had never had a servant like Merlin. He wouldn't take such abuse from anyone else, but somehow he let Merlin get away with it.

'You know, you've got a lot of nerve – for a wimp.'

'I might be a wimp, but at least I'm not a dollop-head.'

Arthur frowned. 'There's no such word, Merlin.'

'It's idiomatic.'

The prince frowned. 'It's what?'

'You need to be more in touch with the people.' Merlin smiled sweetly at him.

Arthur couldn't believe Merlin had resorted to childish name-calling! 'Describe dollop-head.'

'In two words?'

'Yeah.'

'Prince Arthur.'

Arthur barely heard the reply. In the clearing ahead of them he had spotted something. The remains of a camp . . . He held up a gauntleted hand. The scouting party stopped, waiting, listening. At their prince's command they dismounted, tethering their horses and unsheathing their swords. Ordering his men to spread out, Arthur crept slowly forward, every sense on edge. He knelt by the fire, raking through the ash. The remains were still warm. That meant that whoever had lit it was still close by.

He was rising to his feet when the attack came.

Merlin barely had time to think before the bandits swarmed out of the mist-shrouded trees in a tide of blades and bellowing curses. He saw Arthur ward off the crushing blow of his first assailant, but the prince had been taken off guard and off balance.

Merlin leaped from his horse, ready to rush forward and help his master, when a huge beast of a man loomed out of the swirling mist, an unpleasant smile on his face, a huge sword in his hands.

Merlin reacted at once, bringing the blaze of golden magical power from deep within himself, feeling it build behind his eyes.

'*Ech getech ping to!*'

The words burst from him. For a moment it seemed as though the spell had had no effect, but then there was a loud clang and the bandit stared in disbelief at the knife that had flown across the clearing and attached itself to his sword. Merlin watched in satisfaction as more and more metal objects hurtled through the air – until the man's weapon had vanished beneath a jumble of pots, pans and assorted bits of armour. As the confused bandit struggled with his now useless sword, a smiling Merlin turned to help Arthur once more.

The smile slipped from his face as another, even larger man emerged from the undergrowth, this one holding the biggest axe Merlin had ever seen.

Before he could even think about defending himself, the bandit swung the axe through the air and slashed out at him. Merlin jumped backwards, feeling the rush of air as the axe blade missed him by inches. With a roar, the huge man swung the axe again and again, driving Merlin back across the clearing.

As he was forced into the bushes, Merlin scrabbled frantically for something to defend himself with. His hand grasped a fallen branch and he swung it out in front of him, grateful to have a weapon, however crude.

The bandit lopped the top off the branch with a single stroke of his axe. Another swing and the branch was shortened yet further. Another, and Merlin found himself backed against a tree with nothing but a ragged stump in his hand.

Baring his teeth, his attacker raised the axe for the killing blow.

Merlin seized his moment. His eyes flashed with energy.

'*Ceorfax fyll paet treow!*'

The bandit swung the axe with all his strength. Merlin ducked. The axe blade passed within a hair's breadth of his scalp . . . and continued to slice through the trunk of the tree!

Baffled and confused, the man looked up in horror as the tree toppled towards him. Merlin winced as it crashed to the ground, squashing his opponent flat.

He hurried round the fallen tree, desperate to find Arthur. As he re-emerged into the clearing, he saw the prince engaged in a fierce fight with one of their attackers. As Merlin watched, a second bandit crept out of the mist behind them, a broadsword held high above his head. Merlin hurried forward to warn his master, but his foot caught in the tangle of branches from the toppled tree and he crashed heavily to the ground.

He watched in horror as the second man tensed, getting ready to bring his sword crashing down on Arthur's head. A flash of metal in the leaves before him caught his eye. A spear. Without a second thought he reached out with his magic, feeling his eyes blaze as he raised the spear from the ground and sent it slicing across the clearing.

It slammed into the chest of the bandit with a thud. Arthur dispatched his own opponent and turned just in time to see the body crash into the mulch of the forest floor.

Surprised, the prince spun round, trying to locate where the spear had come from, but spied only Merlin, sprawled amongst the branches of the fallen tree.

'We're not playing hide and seek, Merlin!' he bellowed, and launched himself back into the fray.

Merlin glared after him. 'Dollop-head,' he muttered.

Despite the surprise of their attack, the bandits were no match for the well-trained knights and soldiers of Camelot, and soon the forest was silent once more, the bodies of the dead lying still on the damp earth. Arthur stood amongst his men in the centre of the clearing, breathless and exhausted from the ordeal. Merlin pushed his way through the knights towards him. As he approached, a noise in the undergrowth made him start.

Arthur heard it too, drawing his sword once more and motioning to his men to spread out. Slowly they moved across the clearing towards the sound.

Suddenly a figure stumbled out of the bushes, bloodied and filthy, with wild hair and even wilder eyes.

Arthur stared in stunned disbelief.

'Morgana . . .'

Chapter Two

As dusk fell, the sight of the spires and pennants of Camelot above the distant trees lifted the hearts of all in the exhausted scouting party.

All except for Merlin.

For him, every step closer to the castle was a step closer to an unpleasant death at the hands of Uther Pendragon. He had never considered the possibility that they would find Morgana alive and alone. He had always assumed that if they did indeed find her, she would be in the company of Morgause, and that her complicity in the sorceress's plans would be laid bare for all to see.

But now . . . Merlin felt a chill around his shoulders that had nothing to do with the cool evening air. Almost as soon as she had emerged from the forest, Morgana had collapsed into Arthur's arms and fallen into a deep but troubled sleep. That had saved him for the time being, but when she woke, when she was questioned about what had happened on that dreadful night in Camelot, she would point to Merlin as her attacker, as her would-be murderer, and not even Arthur would be able to save him from the king's wrath then.

Merlin just hoped that Uther's justice would be swift and painless.

They entered the main square and dismounted, weary but happy to have been successful in their quest. Arthur watched as Morgana was led towards the castle. She was exhausted, but he had no doubt that Gaius would tend to her.

He glanced over at where Merlin was dismounting inelegantly from his horse. His servant had been uncharacteristically quiet on the journey back to Camelot. The prince gave a smile. He should be thankful for small mercies.

He thrust the reins of his own horse into Merlin's hands. 'You can bring me my supper in my chambers. Then you can get the horses groomed and fed.'

To his surprise Merlin said nothing; normally there would have been a groan of protest at the very least.

'After you've mucked out the stables . . .' he added

mischievously. 'Oh, and cleaned out my room . . . you can polish my armour . . .'

There was still no response from Merlin. Arthur was sure that he wasn't even listening.

'And then I want you to take a pair of scissors and trim the tournament ground . . . to the height of my little finger.'

Merlin continued to stare in a daze at the door to the castle. Arthur had had enough.

'Merlin, are you listening to me?'

Merlin snapped out of his trance. 'What? Yes . . . Of course . . . I look forward to it.'

Arthur couldn't understand his servant sometimes. Their quest was over. They had succeeded.

'Cheer up, Merlin. Morgana's home, and you know what that means . . . ?'

The boy looked at him blankly.

'No more riding on your little bottom . . .'

Merlin didn't even smile.

Morgana lay motionless on the bed, her face as pale as the clean white linen. Gaius studied her carefully. She was exhausted, her eyes red-rimmed with tears and lack of sleep, her jet-black hair dull and matted with dirt. This was a pale shadow of the girl he knew, but with time, and kindness, she would recover.

Her eyes flickered open and she looked at him wearily.

Gaius smiled down at her. 'You need to rest,' he told her.

Morgana gave the faintest of nods, then settled back into the pillows once more.

As the physician gathered his bags, Gwen hurried over to his side. 'I'll stay with her.'

Gaius nodded. 'Call me when she wakes, Guinevere.'

Gwen settled into the chair by Morgana's bed, her eyes never leaving her mistress's face. Gaius smiled. He could think of no one who would take better care of her. He crossed the chamber and slipped out into the corridor, closing the door quietly behind him.

'How is she?' Uther was at his side in a moment.

'She'll be fine.'

'There's nothing wrong with her?' The king sounded anxious.

'Not physically,' Gaius reassured him.

The relief in Uther was palpable, and the tension that had built up over the weeks and months that Morgana had been missing seemed to drain out of him in a rush. 'May I see her?' he asked.

'Best to wait until morning,' said Gaius gently. Morgana was still weak, and the king's enthusiasm at seeing her safe and well might be a little too much for her.

'Of course.' Uther nodded, understanding.

He made to leave, and then stopped, turning back towards the court physician, his face full of gratitude, his voice cracking with emotion. 'Thank you, Gaius . . .'

Gaius watched him go. It was rare for Uther to be so overcome with emotion, rarer still for him to let anyone see it. Gaius had never realized that Morgana was so precious to him. Almost as precious as Arthur . . .

Merlin paced agitatedly around Gaius' chambers, waiting for the old physician to return. When the door finally did open, Merlin all but pounced on him.

'Did you talk to her?' he asked worriedly.

Gaius disentangled himself from the young warlock's grasp. 'She's sleeping.'

'She say anything about me?' Merlin desperately needed to know.

'Nothing as yet.'

Merlin slumped into a chair. 'Well, she's going to.' He was amazed that nothing had yet been said. Every creak of a floorboard, every scuffed footstep had him looking towards the door, expecting the king's guards to have come for him.

'We don't know that,' said Gaius, trying to reassure him.

'She won't have forgotten . . . I tried to kill her. She knows that.' Merlin was thankful that at least Morgana still knew nothing of his powers.

'You had no choice. Either you poisoned Morgana or Camelot fell. You did the right thing.'

Merlin looked at Gaius despairingly. They had been over this time and time again, but nothing could convince the boy that what he had done was for the best. To have her back, knowing what he had done . . . It was worse than if he had killed her. If she had died, then that would have been his burden and he would have taken that secret to the grave.

'But Uther won't know that.' Merlin's expression was glum. 'All she'll say is that I tried to kill her.'

'We can't be sure, Merlin.'

Merlin took a deep breath. 'What do you think Uther will do to me?'

Gaius didn't answer the question. They both knew the answer. 'Let's just wait and see what tomorrow brings.' The old physician tried to look confident, but

Merlin knew him well enough to see the worry in his eyes.

He sighed. It was going to be a long night.

Ultimately it was Gaius who endured the endless night. He had persuaded Merlin to take one of his sleeping draughts – ironically the very ones that he used to prepare for Morgana to help with her bad dreams – and the boy had gone to his bed early, falling into an uneasy sleep.

Gaius had sat in the cool darkness of his chamber, trying to think through the situation in a calm and methodical way, but he feared that Merlin could well be right about the outcome. Uther was certain to react violently to any attack upon his ward, and if Morgana chose to tell him of Merlin's actions, then the boy was doomed. The king would never believe that Morgana would ever act against the interests of Camelot; he would take it as a personal insult even to suggest such a thing.

Like Merlin, he could think of no good reason why Morgana would keep the boy's actions to herself.

When one of Arthur's messengers arrived a little after dawn, it was almost a relief.

Gaius pushed open the door to Merlin's room. The

boy was still asleep. For a moment Gaius was almost of a mind to tell Arthur that Merlin was indisposed, but there was no point in delaying matters any further. He shook Merlin gently by the arm.

'Merlin.'

Merlin stirred groggily.

'Arthur has requested your presence . . .'

The reply was incomprehensible, but the sentiment was clear.

'In Morgana's chambers,' added Gaius.

Merlin was suddenly wide awake. The two stared at each other. It was the moment of truth.

Merlin made his way through the castle in a daze. Everything seemed unreal somehow, as if he were still asleep and all this were still a dream. As he approached Morgana's chambers, he could see that the door was ajar, and he could hear voices from within.

'It all happened so fast . . .'

Merlin's heart was pounding as he strained to hear what Morgana was saying.

'For the second time in as many days, my life changed for ever. We were set upon by bandits and separated. I never saw Morgause again. I have no idea if she is dead or alive.'

Merlin frowned. This was not the conversation that

he expected Morgana to be having. Gingerly he eased open the door and slipped into the room. He could see Arthur sitting at Morgana's bedside, listening as she told her story.

'She cannot hurt you now.' The prince's voice was soothing and gentle.

'I was kept in a cell for almost a year . . . until I'd forgotten what daylight was. I thought I'd go mad.'

Merlin could see Arthur tense, his anger at what had been done to Morgana barely restrained.

'How did you escape?' he asked.

'They moved me. About a week ago.' Morgana shook her head sadly. 'I don't know why. It may have been the patrol from Camelot.'

'The patrol found you?'

'I thought I was going to be free.' Morgana looked at Arthur with despair on her face. 'But then I saw them, killed . . . Every one of them was cut down. There was nothing I could do.'

Tears welled in her eyes. 'But that night the bandits were distracted by their spoils. I took my chance. I ran into the woods. I hid by day and moved by night. When I saw you, I couldn't believe it . . .'

The grief overcame her and she leaned into

Arthur's embrace. The two of them sat silently in each other's arms for a long while. Merlin shuffled nervously, uncomfortable at having to watch such a private moment.

Alerted to his presence, the two of them separated, Morgana wiping the tears from her eyes.

'I think I need to rest.'

Arthur got to his feet, straightening his tunic. 'Everything is going to be all right. You're safe now. If you need someone to be with you . . . If you need anything . . .'

Morgana smiled gratefully at him. 'Thank you.'

Arthur strode past Merlin and out into the corridor. As Merlin turned to follow his master, Morgana called out from the bed.

'Oh, Merlin?'

His heart leaped. Slowly he turned to see Morgana watching him intently.

'I want to speak to you.'

Merlin stole a quick glance at the door. Was Arthur waiting for him? Would he hear what she was about to say? But the prince had gone. Merlin and Morgana were alone.

'I know what you did,' she said coolly.

Time stopped. Merlin couldn't breathe.

'You tried to poison me.'

To hear the truth uttered so bluntly was more than Merlin could bear. 'I didn't want to,' he blurted out, desperate for her to realize what an impossible choice he had been forced to make. Desperate to find the right words.

'It's all right, Merlin. I understand.' Morgana's voice was calm and quiet.

Merlin stared at her, unable to believe what he had just heard.

'You were only trying to protect your friends.' She smiled at him. 'I would've done the same.'

'Really?' His voice was little more than a squeak.

'I was so naïve, Merlin. I don't think I really understood what I was doing. Morgause used me.' She dropped her eyes from his. 'But believe me . . . I've seen the evils of the world. I've seen first hand what it is that Uther fights against. You don't know how much I regret everything I did.'

She looked back at him, her dark eyes soft and gentle. 'I just hope you can forgive me.'

For a moment Merlin could only stare at her: after all he had done, after all he had feared, she was actually asking for *his* forgiveness. He didn't know where to begin with his gratitude.

'I'm sorry for everything you've been through,' he stammered.

Morgana smiled at him; Merlin could do nothing but smile in return. 'It's good to have you back.'

Gaius jumped as Merlin hurried back into the room. He hadn't expected him back so quickly. Come to think of it, he hadn't expected him back at all!

'Merlin!' he exclaimed anxiously. 'Are you all right?'

'I don't know.'

Merlin looked drained, worn out. Galvanized into action by the boy's apparent lack of urgency, Gaius started scurrying around the room, grabbing items and stuffing them into a satchel. 'We'll have to get you out of the city. You'll need food, horses—'

'I'm not going anywhere,' said Merlin bluntly.

'You are if you want to keep that head on your shoulders.' Gaius glared at him sternly. If Morgana was on her way to tell the king of Merlin's deed, then they only had moments. Every second was vital.

'She forgave me . . .'

The old man stared at him, unsure if this was one of Merlin's practical jokes or not. His mind whirled. 'But you poisoned her.'

Merlin gave a weak smile. 'I know.'

Gaius sighed. What could Morgana possibly be up to? There was no way that she could mistake Merlin's actions for an accident . . . 'I don't understand,' he muttered.

'I'm not sure I do either . . .'

The two of them stared at each other in silence. Eventually Gaius spoke.

'What exactly did she say to you, Merlin?' He needed to know what Morgana was up to.

'That what she did was wrong . . . That she's sorry.'

The physician frowned. That sounded like a very convenient solution. 'Do you believe her?'

Merlin shrugged. 'I don't know what to believe.'

Gaius thought hard. 'She has been through a lot this past year . . .' he murmured. Could it really be that simple?

'Maybe she's . . . grown up.' Merlin looked at his mentor hopefully.

'Do you trust her not to tell Uther?' Gaius was stern. This was a dangerous secret for Morgana to keep. It would be so simple to use it against Merlin if she so chose.

Merlin thought for a moment, then nodded. 'Yes, I do . . .'

Gaius seemed to agree with him. 'I suppose that if she was going to tell him, she would have done it by now.'

'Exactly!' Merlin grinned. Suddenly everything was going to be all right. 'You always said that she had a good heart, Gaius.'

Gaius said nothing; he was lost in his own thoughts.

Chapter Three

Arthur's chambers had never looked so clean. The bed was beautifully made, the windows sparkled in the morning sun and Arthur's armour shone almost as brightly.

Merlin was kneeling on the floor, scrubbing at the flagstones, a bucket of soapy water at his side, a stupid smile still spread across his face. As Arthur came in, he looked up and beamed at him.

The prince was immediately suspicious. 'What are you looking so happy about?'

'The sun is shining, we've found Morgana . . .' Merlin clambered to his feet. 'And I've finished all my chores.'

Arthur gave him a despairing look and made to push past him.

Merlin's face fell. 'Do you have to go in there now?'

'Why?' asked Arthur, exasperated.

'I've just washed the floor.' Merlin nodded at the gleaming flagstones.

'Don't worry, I won't slip over.' The prince patted him on the shoulder reassuringly, and strode into the room, a trail of muddy footprints left in his wake.

Merlin gave a sigh of despair. 'You really have no idea, do you?'

Arthur just found his frustration funny. 'All you have to do is wipe it.'

'How would you know?' said Merlin tetchily.

The prince gave him a look of mock indignation. 'I beg your pardon, Merlin?'

'You've never had to do it.' Snatching up the damp rag from the bucket, the boy got back down onto his knees and started wiping away the muddy footprints.

'Oh, I know how to use a mop and bucket,' Arthur said grandly.

'Oh yeah?' Merlin barely gave him a glance.

'It's easy, Merlin. Here, let me show you.'

Arthur reached down and snatched the cloth out of Merlin's hands. Before Merlin could stop him, he slapped the sodden cloth onto the boy's face and grinned. 'You want to see me use a bucket?'

Merlin scrambled to his feet. 'No!'

Resigned to the inevitability of it, he watched as the prince picked up the bucket of dirty water, and tipped it over his servant's head.

On the other side of the castle, Morgana approached the throne room of Camelot. As she reached it, she hesitated for a moment, as if gathering herself; then, with a deep breath, pushed open the heavy doors and stepped inside.

The room was full of councillors and court officials, listening as Sir Leon, one of the most senior of the Knights of Camelot, gave his report to the Council.

'The grain stores are running low, but we are expecting supplies from the northern borders before the end of the week . . .'

He tailed off, aware that attention was no longer on him, but on the raven-haired figure making her way slowly towards the king.

Uther too had spotted her, and rose to his feet, a smile animating his features. 'That's enough,' he announced. 'Leave us.'

Councillors and officials dispersed quickly and without complaint, recognizing the king's need to spend time with his ward. As the last of them left the room, Uther stepped forward and enfolded Morgana in an embrace. When they finally broke apart, both of them had tears glistening in their eyes. Morgana pulled a silk handkerchief from her robes and brushed the tears from the king's cheek.

Uther caught her hand, leading her towards the throne. 'You should sit.'

'No.' Morgana shook her head, as if embarrassed at the thought of sitting on the throne while the king stood. 'That's all that I've done for a year – sit . . . And pray that you hadn't given up on me.'

Uther gripped her hand all the more tightly. 'Never.'

'I don't know why, I wouldn't have blamed you.'

'You're my ward,' he said firmly. 'My responsibility.'

Morgana lowered her head. 'You've done more than any guardian. You've always cared for me, loved me like your own daughter . . .' She looked back into his eyes. 'Yet I've insulted you, defied you, hurt you . . .' She frowned. 'I don't know why you put up with me.'

Uther smiled at her. 'You've been like that since you were a child.'

'Difficult.'

'Arthur was the same.' He shook his head, remembering the two of them as children. 'But I adored you both.'

'I know.' Morgana gripped his hand with hers. 'And I promise that in the future I will show you the love and respect that you deserve.' She leaned forward and kissed him on the cheek.

The king struggled to hide the wave of emotion that threatened to engulf him. 'I cannot tell you how much it means to me to have you back. We must have a celebration. A feast!'

'I look forward to it.'

Morgana released his hand and curtseyed gracefully. 'I will leave you to your Council. Thank you for finding me, Uther. Thank you for never giving up hope.'

She turned and walked back towards the doors of the throne room, her hand curling around the handkerchief that was still wet with Uther's tears. Unseen by the king, a sly smile twitched at the corner of her mouth. A smile that surely boded no good for Uther – or for Camelot.

The day passed long and slow in Camelot. For the first time in a year there were no patrols setting off at the crack of dawn, no urgent messages being relayed to the king from far corners of the kingdom, no soldiers wearily preparing for week upon week of backbreaking travel on horseback. Camelot was slowly settling back into a routine that had almost been forgotten, and when night finally fell over the spires and turrets of the citadel, everything was calm and peaceful.

Morgana slipped out of the castle into the quiet stillness, her slim form shrouded in a heavy cape, her beautiful face hidden by a voluminous hood. She hurried across the moonlit cobbles and into the lower town. As she made her way through the silent streets, the sound of an approaching patrol sent her scurrying to the shadows, but the guards were lax, the evening too quiet and uneventful for them to bother making a thorough inspection, and they passed within feet of her hiding place without so much as a glance in her direction.

Grateful for their carelessness, Morgana hurried to the edge of the town, where a horse stood waiting for her. Climbing effortlessly into the saddle, she spurred her steed into a gallop, vanishing into the forest and becoming one with the shadows.

The forest was alive with night creatures, but Morgana paid them no heed. Anyone from the town foolish enough to venture there at night had all manner of monsters to fear, but she did not allow the threat to trouble her.

She rode for an hour or so, the trees closing in around

her all the while. Finally she brought her horse to a halt. Ahead of her, a sheer wall of rock rose from the mulch of the forest floor, its surface covered with vines and creepers, a ragged set of steep steeps cut into the stone. High above her, firelight flickered from a jagged cave mouth, thin tendrils of oily smoke coiling towards the distant moon.

Morgana slipped off her mount, leaving the skittish animal at the foot of the steep path. As she approached the cave, two figures emerged from the deepening shadows. She stopped in her tracks, looking at the two knights. Their armour was as black as the night sky, their clothes ragged and thick with the stains of battle. A sigil – a blood-red tree on a field of black – stood out like an open wound on their breastplates. The crest of the Bloodguard.

Morgana waited; then, as one, the two knights bowed low. She was expected. Hurrying past them, she swept into the cave.

A lone figure waited for her inside. The slim form was clad in armour, blonde hair cascading down her back in lazy curls. Her soft features were bathed in orange light from the fire, her eyes dancing with reflected flames.

Morgause.

She embraced Morgana as warmly as Uther had done earlier that day. 'My sister,' she said, her voice was warm and low, 'how have you fared?'

'Camelot has welcomed back its daughter with open arms.'

'Uther does not suspect?' Morgause asked warily.

'He laps up my lies like the snivelling dog he is.' Morgana sneered at the weakness she had witnessed in the throne room.

'And the boy?'

'Merlin' – Morgana almost spat the name – 'he believes that I have changed.' Her eyes blazed. 'And he is right. Soon he will see exactly how much.'

She reached into her robes and handed her half-sister the handkerchief that she had used to wipe away Uther's tears.

Morgause's smile was not a pleasant one. 'You've done well.'

She took the piece of silk and held it up to the firelight; then, with a flick of her wrist, cast it into the cauldron that bubbled by the fireside. As the white material touched the surface of the liquid within, it turned black.

'The tears of Uther Pendragon have only begun to fall . . .'

Morgause reached down into an ancient wooden box. When she straightened, she held in her hands a strange shrivelled shape. For a moment, in the dancing firelight, it might almost have been mistaken for some hideous misshapen baby, but as Morgana looked closer she could see that it was a root of some kind. The pale, flesh-like bark was gnarled and twisted with strange, contorted shapes, and long wispy tendrils curled around its extremities like wiry hair.

The sorceress tossed it casually into the cauldron. As the root touched the boiling water, a hideous scream cut through the cavern, part human, part something demonic and terrible. Morgana clasped her hands over her ears. The noise cut through to the very centre of her brain.

Morgause swirled the bubbling liquid with a blackened ladle, staring into the steam that coiled in misty clouds above the fire.

'The mandrake root is very special. Only those with magic can hear its cries,' she murmured. 'But for those without magic, the mandrake pierces the deep recesses of the soul . . . twisting the unconscious into the very image of fear and dread. Uther Pendragon will find that his great kingdom counts for nothing when he has lost his mind.'

She took a deep breath, closing her eyes and

breathing in the vapour. She started to mutter harsh, guttural words under her breath – dark, terrible words from the old religion.

'*Mid pawem wundorcreaft paes ealdan aew ic pe hate niman Utheres wodropa ond pa gemengan mid his blode. Sy he undewitting ond deofolseocnes his heortan afylle . . .*'

Morgause opened her eyes and exhaled slowly. Carefully she lifted the twisted root from the cauldron. Its flesh-like skin was now stained black. Wet and glistening, it steamed slightly as she wrapped it in a cloth.

She handed the bundle to Morgana and the two women stared silently at each other. The end of the reign of Uther Pendragon was upon them.

By the time Morgana had made it back to the castle and set the mandrake root to do its work, it was almost dawn. More than once she had to duck into a storeroom or hide behind an ornamental tapestry in order to get back to her chambers unseen. Now, in the safety of her room once more, she could finally allow herself to relax. Even though she had had no sleep she felt elated, alive, eager to see the results of her night's work.

The root had stained her fingers black, and she

stood at the window, idly washing off the thick sap, wondering what form Uther's madness might take.

There was a cough from behind her. Morgana started, snatching a towel from her washstand to hide the black stains. Merlin stood in the doorway, a bunch of wild flowers in his hands.

'I wanted to say thank you . . .' He smiled that lopsided smile of his. 'What you said yesterday meant a lot.'

Morgana forced herself to take the flowers graciously. 'They're beautiful.'

As she turned to place the flowers on her table, she could see Merlin frowning as he caught sight of the thick black marks that had stained the towel. She cursed inwardly. The boy was a menace!

She caught his arm, steering him back towards the door. 'You're so sweet, Merlin. You've always been such a good friend. I'll have Gwen find a vase.'

For a moment it looked as though Merlin was about to say something, to question the ugly stains that he had seen. Morgana's mind was racing. Suddenly an impatient cry echoed around the corridor outside.

'Merlin!'

Merlin rolled his eyes, but Morgana had never been more thankful to hear Arthur's voice.

'You'd better see what he wants,' she said, forcing a smile to her lips.

Merlin hurried from the room.

Morgana shut the door and stared down at her black hands. In her mind she thought she could hear the cry of the mandrake as it started to do its work.

Chapter Four

Servants surrounded the king as they prepared him for the day. Gaius watched patiently as he was dressed in his finery. The king was in a good mood, and that was a novelty after the past year.

Uther glanced over at his old friend. 'How is Morgana?' he asked.

'She seems to have made a remarkable recovery, sire.' That was certainly true, thought Gaius. It was almost as if her ordeal had never happened.

The king found nothing odd in her fortitude. 'She was like that as a child – very brave. She's inherited much from her father.'

Gaius nodded. 'Gorlois was a great man.'

'Indeed. I trust she will be well enough to attend the feast?'

'I see no reason why not.'

'Thank you, Gaius.'

The king returned to his morning routine, making it clear that Gaius was dismissed. The old physician gave a brief bow of his head and left to attend to his own duties.

Unseen by all of them, in the dark shadows beneath the king's bed, the mandrake root hung, pulsing almost imperceptibly. A single drop of thick liquid gathered itself on the tip of a thin tendril, then splashed down onto the flagstone floor.

On the training grounds within the citadel, the morning sun glinted off the silver armour of the Knights of Camelot, and the air rang with the sounds of swordplay. Arthur stood in the centre of the field, a blindfold across his eyes, his sword held before him. The knights surrounded him in a wide circle, and one by one tried to breach his defences. With each attack he parried or ducked the blows with consummate skill. He was possibly the finest swordsman in the kingdom. Unfortunately he knew it.

'Let's change weapons,' he cried cheerfully.

As the knights withdrew, Merlin hurried forward to remove his blindfold.

'What do you think?' Arthur was pleased with his performance.

Merlin wasn't about to boost his ego. 'I've seen better.'

'Of course.' The smile faded from the prince's face. 'You're an expert at fighting with your eyes closed.'

Merlin shrugged modestly. 'You didn't see what I did when we rescued Morgana.'

'Because you were hiding behind a tree!'

'No I wasn't!' retorted Merlin angrily.

Arthur wasn't listening. 'Merlin, I did think that maybe one day my servant would get used to these situations, and learn to be brave and strong. But after all this time I've come to realize that you'll always be a wimp.'

Merlin had to bite his tongue, aware as always that it was better for all concerned if Arthur remained ignorant of his abilities.

The prince called across to his knights. 'I'm not going to use a blindfold. I'm just going to fight like Merlin.'

He screwed up his eyes and started to stagger comically around the training ground, a look of mock terror on his face. Merlin felt himself flush with embarrassment as the men joined in the prince's laughter.

The knights recommenced their training, only this time with maces against the prince's sword. As they fought, the ground started to become churned up and slippery beneath their feet, and a sudden thought occurred to Merlin. One of the knights was a great ox of a man, useful in a fight, but without the finesse of his fellows. Arthur was warding his attack off easily, but perhaps with a little help . . .

Merlin summoned the power from deep within himself, feeling the blaze of warmth behind his eyes. Checking that no one was watching, he gestured towards the prince just as the huge knight lunged at him.

Arthur's sword spun out of his grasp, and his feet slipped on the wet earth. The knight's mace connected with his breastplate, giving a harsh clang, and the prince went down hard.

Merlin wandered over to where Arthur was floundering in the mud, the breath knocked out of him. The young warlock shook his head sadly.

'I did think that one day my master would learn to be sensitive and tactful, but after all this time I've realized that it will never be. You will always be a dollop-head.'

Arthur glared at him. 'I am not a dollop-head!'

Merlin looked at the prince's mud-caked face and grinned. 'If you say so, sire.'

From her window Morgana watched as Merlin and the knights hauled Arthur to his feet. She felt nothing but contempt for all of them. Silly boys playing at being men. When she was done with Uther, she would take the greatest of pleasure in teaching them that life was not all about games.

But Merlin . . . he in particular would pay for what he had tried to do. She could still remember the harsh burning in her throat as the hemlock had started to do its work; could still recall the agonizing pain that had raced through her veins as she struggled to draw breath. She had nearly died, and it had taken all Morgause's skill and magic to save her.

Merlin would suffer for that. He would relive her agony a thousand times over before he died. She would see to that personally.

A feast was a source of huge excitement in Camelot. It had been so long since there had been a celebration like this that most of the huge kitchen ovens had gone cold with lack of use. For days there had been a steady stream of servants carrying wood they'd gathered from the forest to stoke the fires properly.

As the fires raged, food from across the kingdom had been prepared, everyone determined that the feast celebrating Morgana's return to Camelot would be one remembered for years to come.

The banqueting hall was alive with music and loud conversation, knights in brightly coloured cloaks mingling with courtiers and servants. Uther sat at the top table, flanked by his son and his ward and their servants, a half-eaten plate of meat in front of him, a huge flagon of wine in his hand.

He rose to his feet, thumping the flagon down on the table, sending wine splashing everywhere. The boisterous babble descended to a respectful hush.

'Standing here, seeing so many happy faces,' said Uther, swaying a little unsteadily, 'it seems almost like a dream. I can tell you, it's been a long time since I've felt like this.'

'What – drunk?' cried Arthur. Laughter rippled around the hall.

Uther beamed at his son. 'Drunk with happiness!'

He looked over to where Morgana was smiling up at him.

'I would have searched the entire world – the sea, the sky, the stars – for that smile. To have that stolen

from me, it was like a blade to my heart. Morgana . . .'
He shook his head. 'There are no words . . . You mean
more to me than you will ever know.'

He raised his goblet. 'To the Lady Morgana!'

The hall erupted with cheers. Morgana got to her
feet and embraced Uther tightly. He held her tight for a
moment, then extricated himself from her arms, a frown
creasing his brow.

'I need some air.'

Morgana watched as the king made his way through
the happy revellers and out into the cool night air.

She felt a surge of anticipation. It had started.

Uther stumbled unsteadily down the great stone staircase into the courtyard. Arthur was right: he *was* drunk,
or at least closer to being drunk than he had been for a
very long time. He needed something to help steady his
swirling senses.

He stopped at the foot of the steps, breathing deeply,
taking in great lungfuls of fresh air. He could not remember a time when he had felt more content. The last year
had drained him, made him weak. Now that Morgana
was back where she belonged, he could rule without
fear again.

A noise from across the courtyard made him look up.

A scratching sound. He could see nothing. The square was empty. Uther turned to rejoin the feast when the sound came again, louder and more strident this time.

'Who is that?' The king's voice echoed off the white stone walls. 'Arthur?'

There was no response, just the slightest rustle of the wind through the distant treetops. Uther ran a hand across his brow. He really had drunk more than he ought.

The scratching came again. Insistent. Persistent. He frowned. He wasn't imagining it: there was something there. He strained to pinpoint where the noise was coming from. It seemed to emanate from the well on the far side of the square.

Pulling his cloak around him, Uther crossed the courtyard in swift strides. Good mood or not, if someone saw fit to play foolish games with him, they would regret it. And drunk or not, he was still the king and would not countenance any disrespect.

He reached the well and peered into it. Moonlight glinted off the shimmering water, but otherwise it was empty. Puzzled, Uther leaned closer, trying to find the source of the noise.

Without warning, a hand slid out of the cold

black water, clamping around his wrist. It was a woman's hand, thin and elegant, the skin pale to the point of translucency. Uther gasped at the vice-like grip. The hand was cold, clammy, and immensely strong. He struggled to free himself, too shocked even to cry out.

The water swirled and heaved and, with a horrible noise like the last breath of a dying man, a face emerged from the well.

Uther stared in horrified disbelief. The woman was pale, deathly pale, her fine blonde hair plastered to her scalp. As water trailed from her nose and mouth in thin rivulets, he realized with sudden dread that it was a face he knew all too well.

Ygraine, who had been his beloved wife. Ygraine, the mother of his son. Ygraine, the woman whom he had so badly betrayed.

Ygraine – who had died nearly eighteen years ago.

All reason left him, and he started to struggle violently in her grip, desperate to be free. With a vile bubbling, Ygraine opened her mouth, a single word bursting from her lips.

'Please . . .'

Uther screamed.

Chapter Five

'Here . . .'

Morgana drew back the covers of the king's bed. Arthur and Merlin carried the unconscious Uther into the room and laid him gently down on the mattress.

'Careful.'

Morgana pulled the blankets up around him tenderly. The guards had found him slumped against the wall near the well, hands curled tight around his head, eyes wide with fear. It had taken a dozen of them to persuade him to stand, a dozen more to get him back into the castle so that his physician could attend to him. Gaius could make no sense of what the king had said and had administered a strong sleeping draught.

The old man watched as Uther drifted into an uneasy sleep, his mind whirling with suspicions.

'Is he going to be all right?' asked Morgana, interrupting his musings.

'He should sleep until morning.'

She turned back to her guardian, stroking his wrist gently. Gaius ushered the others from the room. As the door closed, Morgana let Uther's hand drop from her grasp, a secret smile on her lips.

Everything was going to plan.

Merlin followed Arthur and Gaius out of the king's chamber. Outside, the prince was anxiously questioning the physician about his father's condition.

'What could have made him like this?'

Gaius had his suspicions. True, he had never seen the king behave in this way, but he had seen the symptoms before . . . a very long time ago. 'I've no idea,' he said.

'Gaius, he was lying on the floor crying!' Arthur exclaimed. Gaius had never seen him so concerned.

'Tiredness.' The old man was in no mood to share his suspicions with the prince. Not yet. Not until he was sure. He started to walk back towards his own chambers.

'Gaius!' Arthur cried after him. The despair in his voice made the physician stop. He looked at the prince guiltily, knowing that Arthur could see he was holding something back.

'What aren't you telling me?' asked the prince. 'What's wrong with him? . . . Tell me!'

Gaius took a deep breath. 'When I found him, he was mumbling. Most of it was incoherent, but . . .'

'What?'

'He kept mentioning your mother's name.'

Arthur looked as though he had been slapped. 'He never talks about her,' he said quietly.

'He claimed that he saw her.' Gaius hesitated for a moment, then added, 'In the well.'

Merlin could see that Arthur was stunned, his face creased with puzzlement.

'He'd had a lot of wine.' Gaius tried to keep his tone reassuring. 'Such hallucinations are not uncommon.'

'Did the guards see the king in this state?' Arthur's concerns were beginning to parallel Gaius' own. A soldier expected his leader to be fearless, strong of mind . . .

'I think that you're worrying too much.' Gaius did his best to keep the prince calm.

'If the people get to know about this—'

'We'll say he was ill,' Gaius cut across him, 'but that he's now recovered.'

Arthur nodded, but Gaius realized that Merlin had seen through the soothing words all too clearly.

All the way back to his chambers Gaius had remained silent. Even now, in the quiet and privacy of his old book-filled room he was just sitting deep in thought, a book on his lap. Merlin could tell that he was deeply concerned.

'You don't really think that it was the drink, do you?' There was more to Uther's ravings than a few glasses of wine – that much was obvious even to Merlin.

'I'm reading,' snapped Gaius, turning a page of his book, unwilling to be drawn into a conversation.

'Try using your eyeglasses.' Merlin knew that the old man couldn't see properly without his battered old pair of spectacles. He certainly couldn't read without them.

Gaius shot him a look, aware that he'd been caught out. He rummaged around on the table. 'Where are they?'

Merlin perched the glasses on the end of his nose and peered at the blur that Gaius had become. How did he see anything through these? The old man spotted him and snatched the glasses back.

'Merlin, this is serious!'

'So, are you going to tell me?' Merlin knew it was serious, and wasn't going to let Gaius off without knowing more of his suspicions.

Gaius put on his glasses and slumped back in his chair. 'Since Morgana's disappearance the king's mental state has grown increasingly fragile.'

Merlin frowned at him. 'What are you saying?'

Gaius shot a wary look at the door and dropped his voice. 'I fear Uther is losing his mind . . .'

Merlin was shocked. A sane Uther was dangerous enough; with his judgement impaired he could be capable of almost anything.

Far from Camelot, in a cave set high in a cliff face, Uther was the subject of another conversation, one less concerned with his wellbeing.

'It is happening just as you said.' Morgana was breathless from both her ride and the exhilaration she felt. 'Already the rumours are spreading.'

Morgause looked pleased. 'The mandrake's poison does its work well.'

'Better than I had dared to hope. Soon all of Camelot will believe that the king is going mad.'

'And a kingdom without a king is ripe for the picking.'

Morgana's eyes shone. 'When do you go to Cenred?'

'Tomorrow.'

'And he will do as we wish?'

'Cenred wishes only to please me.' Morgause smiled coquettishly, all too aware of the effect that she could have if she so desired.

Morgana caught her meaning. 'Then your time with him has been well spent.'

Her sister threw another mandrake root into the cauldron, its screams drowning out their laughter.

Morgana had almost made it back to the castle drawbridge when the patrol appeared. Cursing her luck, she ducked into the shadows, hardly daring to breathe, aware that if they looked in her direction, then there was no way that they could fail to see her.

The soldiers passed by and Morgana breathed a sigh of relief. Since Uther had fallen ill Arthur had increased the number of patrols, as much to ensure that groups of gossiping villagers were dispersed quickly as for security.

She stepped out of the shadows, ready to make her way back to her chambers, when a voice from behind her made her freeze.

'Lady Morgana?'

A lone sentry, probably one about to take up duties on the battlements, was crossing the courtyard towards her. Morgana felt a surge of panic. She had been careless. Her mind was full of the pact that she had struck with Morgause, the path that she was setting herself, the changes that it would bring . . .

'I was just taking a stroll,' she stammered.

To her dismay she realized that the guard was staring at her cloak.

'What's that, my lady?' he asked.

Morgana glanced down to see a large dark stain spreading across the expensive fabric. Sap from the mandrake root! In the cold light of the moon the thick, viscous liquid looked just like blood.

'You're bleeding.' The sentry hurried forward, eager to help.

'I'm fine, really.' Morgana tried to push past him, unwilling to be involved in a fight to protect her secret so soon, but the guard was not easily convinced.

'You're wounded. Let me see . . .'

He pulled back her cloak, stepping back in surprise at the sight of the gargoyle-like shape of the mandrake root in its dark, wet cloth. Black sap splashed noisily onto the cobblestones.

In that moment Morgana knew that any last chance of retreating from the choice she had made was gone. All hope of redemption ebbed from her as she drew the dagger out of her belt.

With a lightning blow honed from years of watching Arthur and his knights, she plunged the blade into the chest of the unsuspecting sentry.

For a moment the man stared disbelievingly, almost comically, at the dagger protruding from his chest; then, with a choked cry, he toppled over the edge of the drawbridge, his body vanishing into the blackness. There was a sickening thump as he hit the rocks far below.

Morgana stood there for a moment, staring at the blood that stained her hands, as if unsure of what it was that she had just done, then hastily wiped it away on her cape. It had never been her intention to kill. She wasn't some common murderer, but she had had no choice. If she had been discovered now, with Morgause's plan barely started . . .

Pulling her cloak around her, she hurried towards her chambers, desperate to be safely away from prying eyes. Slipping into her room, she placed the mandrake root carefully in an ornate chest, covering it with the black cloth. She pulled off her gloves and cloak. Both were stained with sap and mud and blood. She needed to get rid of them before morning.

There was a soft knock at her door. Quickly she bundled the soiled garments together and thrust them under her bedcovers. Gwen's tired face appeared at the doorway. Her servant smiled warmly, obviously woken from her sleep, but still happy to serve her mistress.

'I saw the light. I wanted to make sure that you were all right.'

'I'm fine.' Morgana was aware of the sharpness in her tone.

'You're still dressed,' Gwen said, looking puzzled.

'I'll prepare for bed myself.'

Gwen hovered at the doorway, uncertain as to what she should do. 'Are you sure?'

'That will be all, Gwen,' snapped Morgana, her voice cold.

Gwen gave a brief curtsey and left the room, the hurt on her face plain.

Unconcerned, Morgana filled a bowl with water and started to wash her hands, watching as the sap of the mandrake and the blood of the guard turned the water as black as night.

Chapter Six

Any hope that Uther would be cured after a good night's sleep seemed to have been a vain one, thought Merlin. The king was pacing around his bedchamber, his hair unkempt, his chin dark with stubble, and a wild look in his eyes.

'It was Ygraine, damn you!' he bellowed.

Gaius did his best to calm him. 'That's impossible, sire.'

'I know my own wife, Gaius,' Uther growled dangerously.

'But she is dead.' Gaius said the words without emotion, trying to impress upon Uther the folly of what he was saying. It had no effect.

'She was here, I tell you,' insisted the king. 'I felt Ygraine's hand. She was so cold, Gaius. So cold and so frightened.'

He gripped Gaius' arm tightly. 'D'you understand?' he hissed in his ear. 'It was her.'

The physician glanced over at Merlin. The king caught the look, and anger clouded his already troubled features. 'Do not doubt me, Gaius.'

Gaius tried to extricate himself from the painful grasp. 'There are a number of possible explanations for these kinds of delusions. Perhaps you've ingested something, sire . . .'

'I saw her . . . I felt her . . .'

'Or it could have been brought on by a fever . . .'

Aware that he was not convincing anyone, Uther relaxed his grip and Gaius rubbed at his bruised arm and made to usher Merlin from the room.

'It's important that you rest now, sire . . .' he told the king.

Uther barely acknowledged him. 'She was here. I swear it. I saw her.'

Glad to be away from the king, Gaius bustled away down the corridor. Merlin hurried to catch up with him.

'What if he did?' he asked.

Gaius remained silent.

'He seemed pretty certain.'

The old physician still said nothing, but Merlin wasn't about to give up. 'He could be telling the truth.'

'Did you see anything last night?' asked Gaius tetchily.

'No.'

'Nor did anyone else.'

He hurried away. The young warlock watched him go. Gaius was worried, very worried, but Merlin wasn't so sure that he was right. Uther was many things, but he was not prone to flights of fancy. It may not have been his long dead wife that he had seen, but he had certainly seen something. Something that had terrified him.

Something was going on, Merlin was certain of it.

He sighed. Still, until he had something more concrete to follow up, there seemed to be little choice other than to carry on with his chores as normal. And that meant cleaning Arthur's armour.

It was hours later when Merlin finally staggered into Arthur's chamber, his arms piled high with the freshly polished armour. Arthur was sitting on his bed, gazing at nothing.

'All finished,' said Merlin. 'Good as new.'

The prince didn't even look up at him.

Merlin let the armour crash heavily onto the table and looked at the prince, puzzled. Usually that would have elicited some reprimand.

'Don't you want to check it?'

'No,' said Arthur. 'Carry on.'

'But you always want to check it.' Merlin frowned. 'You always make me do it at least three times.'

'I'm sure it's fine.'

The boy paused. Arthur could be selfish, thoughtless perhaps, but the two of them had been through a lot together, and Merlin regarded him as a friend. It pained him to see the prince so despondent. He wanted to say something, but knew from bitter experience that his observations were not always welcome.

'He will be all right, you know,' he ventured.

Arthur looked up at him now, expectation in his eyes. 'Has Gaius told you what's wrong?'

Merlin shuffled uncomfortably, unwilling to tell Arthur Gaius' suspicions. 'He's just feeling a bit under the weather.'

As reassurances went it was pretty feeble, and Arthur knew it. The hope faded from his face. 'He's losing his mind, Merlin.'

The boy searched around in his head for something

useful to say. 'Everyone gets a bit . . . you know . . . from time to time . . .'

'In his last years the same thing happened to his father,' the prince said bluntly.

Merlin stayed silent. Gaius had told him as much. Perhaps the king was going mad. 'I suppose it can run in families,' he mused.

Arthur glared at him. 'Is that supposed to make me feel better?'

'No . . .' Merlin could have kicked himself. 'I didn't mean—'

'Because if it is, it's not working!'

Merlin struggled to clamber out of the hole he had dug himself. 'You're still young . . . I mean, you've got years ahead of you . . . before—'

'Merlin,' the prince snapped.

'Yes?'

'Get out.'

'Or?'

Arthur rose from the bed and picked up a piece of armour from the table. 'Or I'm going to throw this piece of armour at your head.'

'Right.' Merlin made a dash for the door, diving through it just as the armour bounced off the door frame, clattering noisily to the floor. He hurried away.

His attempts at cheering up the prince hadn't been entirely without result. At least Arthur was treating him normally again.

The soldiers of the Bloodguard rode fast across the Great Plains, their ragged cloaks streaming behind them, flapping wildly, making them look like some vast flock of predatory birds. At their head rode Morgause, her face clouded with anger, spurring her horse forward.

Soon a vast castle rose up before them, great blocks of grey stone surging into the overcast sky. Morgause slowed her pace, leading her party in through the castle gates. The bailey was full of soldiers of fortune preparing weapons and saddling horses. A few glanced up at the beautiful sorceress and her black-clad retinue as they passed, but most ignored them, intent on their work.

Morgause slipped from her horse, striding into the castle's keep. The Bloodguard followed, hands never far from the hilts of their swords. The sorceress made her way through torch-lit corridors, ignoring cries of protest and challenges, pushing guards aside and forcing her way into the throne room.

A man sat upon the throne before her. Cenred, king of the lands to the east of Camelot. It was a dangerous kingdom, one that lived by the sword rather than by the rule of law. The king's guards were suddenly tense and alert as Morgause approached. Cenred held up a calming hand, staying his men and rising to meet the sorceress as she strode down the throne room towards him.

'To what do I owe this pleasure?' He held his arms wide in greeting.

'If you will not leave your castle, then I must come to you.' Morgause didn't attempt to hide the anger in her voice.

Cenred gave an amused sniff. 'I see you have lost none of your audacity.'

'I wish I could say the same,' sneered Morgause. 'But I find the great King Cenred cowering in his chambers when he should have met me at the border. Perhaps he has lost his nerve. Perhaps he is a coward.'

One of Cenred's guards snatched at his sword, quick to defend the honour of his king. Morgause's eyes flashed with blazing amber light and the knight was hurled across the room, slamming into a wooden table and shattering it to matchwood. He landed in a crumpled heap on the floor.

As one, the Bloodguard drew their swords, stepping close to their priestess. Cenred's men drew their own swords, eager to join the battle, but once again their king raised his hands to stay them and they lowered their weapons.

A smile played around the king's lips. He leaned close to Morgause. 'You're very beautiful when you're angry,' he whispered.

Morgause brushed a strand of hair from her forehead. 'Is that why you continue to defy me?'

Cenred shrugged. 'You wouldn't like it if I made it easy for you.'

Further west, the gathering of mercenaries in the kingdom of Cenred had not gone unnoticed. Uther and Cenred were old enemies. When word had reached Uther of the growing threat, he had called for a meeting of the Council. Now, in the council chamber of Camelot, Arthur was briefing them on what his scouts had told him.

'We've had reports that mercenaries are streaming into Cenred's kingdom,' he announced to the assembled councillors.

Uther frowned. Cenred had never been openly hostile towards them without good reason. It seemed strange that the situation had changed. 'Do we know why?'

'There is a rumour that Cenred is amassing an army.'

Arthur sounded very worried. 'I think we should send a patrol out to assess the situation . . .'

Uther was listening to the prince's words, but they faded into the background as he suddenly became aware of a figure standing against the far wall of the council chamber. He felt his heart begin to pound. Arthur was staring at him . . .

'Father . . . ?'

Uther ignored him. His skin was suddenly cold. He gripped the arms of the throne tightly, unwilling to believe what he was seeing. The figure on the far side of the room was a young boy, no more than eight years old. His skin was glistening and pale, the colour of a dead fish, his hair wet and plastered to his head. Water poured from his clothes, from his fingers, spreading across the floor of the council chamber.

'*Father . . . ?*'

Uther was vaguely aware of his son speaking to him again, but his head echoed with the *drip, drip, drip* of water on the stone floor, and he could not tear his eyes away from the terrified, accusing face of the boy. He knew that he had seen that face before. His mind was full of another time – a time when he could still hear the cries for mercy from the boy's mother.

'Leave me alone!' he spat.

The boy stared impassively back at him, water trickling from his mouth, the pool at his feet getting wider and wider.

'*Get out of here!*' screamed the king, staggering to his feet and sending the throne crashing from the dais. He was aware of Arthur reaching out for him, of the worried cries of knights and courtiers, but he could not tear his gaze away from the pale, accusing child.

Uther tore himself free of Arthur's grasp. 'I said *get out*!' he shrieked, his voice hoarse with fear. 'I will have you hanged!'

The child continued to stand and stare, implacable, impossible. Uther felt the screams welling up inside him, constricting his throat, making him gasp for air. He made to lunge at the boy, but suddenly there were strong hands grasping at his arms, his shoulders. Sir Leon and the prince tried to hold him back, but Uther fought against them, desperate to reach his tormentor. Finally fear and exhaustion sapped his strength and he was dragged sobbing from the council chamber.

Chapter Seven

Merlin had to admit that he was shaken. If there was one thing that he had always known about Uther Pendragon, it was that he was a man in control of himself. Even in the direst of circumstances, the cool calculation of the man was one of his most notable attributes; he remained calm and collected in the face of danger and adversity.

To have seen him so wild and agitated . . . He had been like . . . Merlin grimaced. Like a madman.

Arthur and Sir Leon had carried the struggling king to his chambers and shut him into his room, allowing no one but Gaius to see him. The prince had returned to the council chamber to try and calm the agitated chatter and quell the rumours, but Merlin had already seen how fast news of the king's latest episode had started to spread through the castle. The people knew that Uther was a sick man, and it was unsettling them.

The door to the king's rooms opened and a troubled-looking Gaius stepped out into the corridor. Merlin hurried over to him, eager to know what had happened. The old physician kept his voice low, mindful of prying eyes and ears.

'He saw a young boy, his clothes dripping with water.'

'Who was he?' whispered Merlin.

'There *was* no boy, Merlin,' Gaius reminded him. 'You were there.'

Merlin sighed. Gaius was right. There had been no boy, no water.

Gaius caught him by the arm and led him away from the door. 'In the Great Purge, Uther drowned many he suspected of sorcery. And some, God help them, were children – killed for the magic they were born with.'

Merlin said nothing. He knew only too well about Uther's obsession – about the death that had faced those whom he suspected of sorcery. He was lucky that he had been born after the Great Purge, and far from Camelot, otherwise he could well have been one of those poor, drowned children.

'Maybe his conscience is playing tricks on him,' said

Gaius, but his voice showed that he was as unconvinced as Merlin by his words. 'Whatever it is, we can no longer hide this.'

'You sound concerned.' Merlin had been through much with Gaius, but he had never seen him quite like this. The old man seemed greatly troubled by Uther's condition.

'A king's hold on his people is a fragile thing,' explained Gaius. 'If they lose faith in him, then I fear for Camelot.'

As if cued by his words, the warning bell rang out from the battlements.

Almost as soon as the bell had sounded a guard had arrived, summoning Gaius to the moat. Merlin had followed the two of them deep into the bowels of the castle, eventually emerging through a small door onto the rocks that littered the ground below the drawbridge. Sir Leon was waiting for them.

High overhead Merlin could see worried faces peering down at them. Splayed out on the rocks, one arm at an unnatural angle that could only mean a broken bone, was the body of a guard. He was lying immobile on one of the larger rocks, and there was something sticking out of his chest. As he approached,

Merlin realized with shock that it was the hilt of a dagger.

Gaius hurried over to the man, examining him with experienced hands. It seemed like a pointless exercise to Merlin: no one could have survived a fall like that, even without a dagger in the chest.

As Gaius looked more closely at the knife, he suddenly went pale. Merlin's heart skipped a beat. Surely things couldn't get any worse?

The physician straightened, his face grave. 'Take this man to my chambers,' he said coldly. 'I need to speak with Arthur as a matter of urgency.'

When Morgana received the summons to the council chamber, she had felt elated. Surely this was the news that she had been waiting for: the news that Uther's condition had worsened. If so, then it meant that the second mandrake was working even faster than the first.

When she arrived at the chamber, Gaius was standing before Arthur and his knights and the assembled councillors. She had to hide her delight. The news must be grave indeed to have prompted the calling of such a meeting.

As Gaius began to speak, however, her elation gave way to mounting unease. The body of the guard she had killed had been discovered. She tried to remain calm. After all, there was nothing that could link the body to her, and no reason for anyone to even suspect that she might be involved.

'The sentry must have been attacked at some point during the night . . .' Gaius had almost finished making his report.

'Who could have done this?' Arthur was angry and upset at the death of one of the men in his charge.

Gaius removed a small bundle from his robes. As he unwrapped it, Morgana saw that it was her dagger. Her heart began to pound again, so loudly that she swore it would be heard.

The old man pointed at a design on the hilt – a red tree on a black background. 'That is the sigil of the Bloodguard.'

'The Bloodguard?' Arthur's brow creased, unfamiliar with the name.

'Warrior priests, sworn to protect the high priestesses of the old religion.'

Arthur shook his head, disbelieving. 'But surely they were wiped out in the Great Purge?'

'Not all of them,' said Gaius solemnly.

The prince leaned forward. 'So you believe that there's a traitor in Camelot?'

'It's possible, sire. The sentry will be able to tell us soon enough.'

'He's still alive?' Arthur was incredulous.

'Indeed.'

Morgana's vision darkened. For one dreadful moment she thought that she might faint there and then in front of the whole Council. The sentry was alive!

She left the council chamber in a daze. She had failed. Her treachery would be unmasked. She knew that when her part in all this was revealed, she would be shown no mercy. She was already as good as dead unless she acted quickly.

Far to the east, in the throne room of Cenred's castle, a fire roared in the great stone fireplace. The room was empty now, save for two figures silhouetted against the blaze. A king and a sorceress.

Cenred refilled Morgause's goblet with wine and regarded her suspiciously. 'I'm certain that you have not come all this way to drink, Morgause.'

She sipped at her wine. 'You know me well.'

'Extremely well.' Cenred nodded sagely. 'And yet somehow we're still close.'

The sorceress lowered her goblet. 'I've come to talk to you about our old friend Uther Pendragon.'

'Yes, I've heard the sad news.' The king took a gulp of his own wine. 'He's finally lost his mind.'

'Camelot is weak,' Morgause hissed. 'Weaker than it's been for years. The kingdom is vulnerable, just as I promised.'

Cenred regarded her carefully, fully aware of what she was suggesting. 'Yet it doesn't change the fact that the citadel is impregnable.'

She leaned back in her chair. 'So, even without his wits, Uther is too strong for you.'

The king snorted, unwilling to be goaded. 'You're a woman of great courage, Morgause, but I don't think with my sword. An assault on Camelot cannot be undertaken lightly.'

She swirled the wine in her goblet. 'You forget, we have an ally in the court . . .'

Cenred had heard promises like this before. 'That is no guarantee. Traitors blow like the wind.'

'Not this one.' Morgause's eyes were cat-like in the roaring firelight. 'She can be relied upon until the end – you can be certain of that . . .'

Morgana slipped through the corridors of Camelot like a ghost. Since childhood she had played in the long, dark passageways and secret rooms of the citadel. Arthur was the only person who knew the castle as well as she did; but Arthur had never been able to best her at the games they played.

Tonight, though, the game that she played was a deadly one, a game that could cost her her life if she failed. This was no spur-of-the-moment decision. This was different. This was cold-blooded murder and she knew it. In order to succeed in her plans, she was having to cross unimaginable boundaries.

She made her way up the twisting stone staircase to Gaius' chambers, knocking lightly on the heavy wooden door. 'Gaius? Merlin?'

She peered into the musty, book-filled room. It was dark and silent. Quietly she slipped inside.

The wounded sentry lay on a low bed on the far side of the room. As she stole through the darkness towards him, he stirred in his sleep and moaned, as if aware that the one who had tried to kill him had returned to finish the job.

Morgana stopped next to the shelves of potions and tonics that were the stock of Gaius' trade. Her hand hovered next to a small bottle emblazoned with a skull. Hemlock. The very poison that Merlin had used on her. How fitting.

She took the bottle and stared down at the sleeping

guard, suddenly hesitant about her task. Was the man's survival a sign, a second chance for her to turn back? A last chance at redemption?

She hardened her heart. Uther had set her down this path; he would be responsible for the deaths that led to its conclusion. She opened the bottle.

Wearily, Merlin and Gaius made their way back towards their chambers. The day had taken its toll on both of them. If they had been more alert, they might have noticed the figure that slid into the shadows as they approached the stairs, might have caught the faint sound of footsteps on the flagstoned corridor as they climbed the steps to the physician's quarters; but they were tired, their minds on other things, and the figure passed them unseen.

The instant Merlin pushed open the old wooden door, however, he knew that something was wrong. The room was silent. Completely silent. No sound of breathing, no rustle of sheets or pillows. Gaius' patient lay motionless, his eyes open and staring. Deathly still.

Merlin hurried over to him. 'Gaius!'

The physician rushed to Merlin's side, feeling for a pulse in the guard's neck. He frowned, and in that instant Merlin knew that the man was dead.

'You said he was recovering.'

'I thought he was.'

'Then what happened?'

Gaius had no answer. He pulled a sheet over the dead man's face.

'You don't think it's strange?' asked Merlin.

'Very.'

The two of them regarded each other silently. The guard's death was no accident. The traitor in their midst was cunning. Cunning, dangerous and deadly.

Chapter Eight

The moon rose high over Camelot, the white stone of the castle almost glowing in the night air.

Merlin entered the king's chambers carrying the potion that Gaius had prepared. The old physician was endeavouring to find out how the sentry had died, to see if he could find some clue as to the traitor's identity.

Merlin wished that he understood what this mysterious Bloodguard sought to gain by infiltrating the castle in this way. There was a plan, of that he was sure, and he would be very surprised if it wasn't tied to the king's illness in some way. But he had no proof, and without proof he was helpless.

He glanced over at the slumbering king. The bed was rumpled and untidy. Uther was obviously not sleeping well. As Merlin bent down to pick up the covers, he noticed a dark stain on the white silk. Puzzled, he reached out and touched it. It was wet, sticky. He rubbed the dark liquid between his fingertips. He had seen a stain like this only the other day, on the towels in Morgana's chambers . . .

He looked closer. There was more of the dark goo spattered on the floor. With a sense of growing unease, Merlin bent to try and find the source of the black liquid. As he did so, he heard footsteps hurrying along the corridor outside and stopping outside the door.

Without thinking, Merlin dropped to the floor and rolled under the bed. The door to the king's bedchamber creaked open and someone crept into the room.

He watched as feet crossed to the bedside. As they approached, he shrank back further under the bed, and something wet and sticky brushed against his cheek. Merlin recoiled in disgust. A twisted shape hung in the shadows, held against the bed frame with twine. It was revolting – a mass of gnarled roots that looked like a twisted baby, slick with black slime.

To Merlin's shock, a delicate hand reached down under the bed, groping towards the root. He breathed in hard as it came within a hair's breadth of his face. Fingers grasped the sticky root and pulled it free. Task accomplished, the feet retreated back across the room. Immediately Merlin crawled forward, eager to see who it was.

In the light from the open door the slender figure was unmistakable.

Merlin frowned in confusion.

It was Morgana.

Scrambling out from under the bed, Merlin hurried after her. What on earth was she up to, and what was the root that she had taken from underneath the king's bed? He knew that she possessed magic, but was she really so foolish as to use an enchantment to try and cure him? It didn't make any sense.

He watched though the crack in the door as she crept silently down the passageway, the revolting root hidden in the folds of her cape.

Keeping a safe distance, he followed her through the castle and out into the great courtyard. The night was cold and Merlin wished that he'd had time to get a cape of his own, but he daren't lose sight of Morgana.

Always in the shadows, he tailed her through the lower town, hiding in doorways, behind carts. At one point she stopped, turning suddenly, and Merlin was certain she had caught sight of him as he dived behind a pile of barrels. He crouched motionless, but there was no cry of alarm, no sound of running feet. Morgana hadn't seen him.

He peered carefully from his hiding place. She was standing in the shadows, listening for sounds of pursuit. Merlin felt a jolt of shock as a shaft of moonlight cut across her face. Her eyes blazed; her entire bearing was almost feral, like a hunted animal. This wasn't the Morgana he knew – the gentle, beautiful girl who had been so kind to him when he first arrived in Camelot. What was happening to her?

As he watched, Morgana pulled up the hood of her cape and hurried away towards the edge of town. She was heading for the Darkling Wood. For a moment Merlin hesitated. The wood was no place to be after sundown. As Morgana vanished into the darkness, he realized that he had no choice. He had to know what she was up to.

With a shiver that had nothing to do with the cold, Merlin hurried after her.

Gaius watched as two guards carried the body of the dead sentry away for burial, and was surprised to see the tall figure of Sir Leon in the doorway. The knight was not a regular visitor to the physician's chambers; in fact, Gaius could not think of a single occasion when he had come to visit before.

Sir Leon waited until the guards were well out of earshot, then turned to Gaius, his handsome face creased with worry.

'The people are talking. They are convinced that the king has lost his mind,' he said. He was deeply troubled, and Gaius realized that it must have taken a lot of courage for him to come here and speak in this manner about his king.

'This is nothing but rumour.' Gaius hoped to put his mind at ease, but Sir Leon was not easily persuaded.

'You think his behaviour is rational?'

Gaius said nothing.

Sir Leon leaned close. 'You know as well as I do he is not able to continue his reign,' he whispered.

It was a blunt assessment of the situation, but Gaius refused to accept that Uther was beyond help.

'He needs time.'

'We don't have it,' exclaimed the knight. 'He is the king – his judgement needs to be impeccable. The knights I've spoken to no longer trust him.'

Gaius was startled. If even the king's most trusted men were starting to doubt him, then the situation had become serious sooner than he had hoped.

'They want you to talk to the prince,' Sir Leon continued. 'They want Arthur to assume power.'

'Arthur is not ready,' snapped Gaius. 'He is still young.'

'I know him better than any man. I've fought by his side many times and he's proved himself a great leader.'

'In battle, yes.' Gaius shook his head. 'But does he have the maturity for affairs of state?'

'Gaius, the people are restless.' The knight's tone was pleading now. 'Cenred is amassing an army on our border. The kingdom is looking weak. We have no choice – you must speak to Arthur.'

Gaius thought hard, knowing that what Sir Leon said was right. Uther was in no fit state to lead his army into battle. Ready or not, it was time for Arthur to take on the burden of leadership.

Merlin followed Morgana through the eerie blackness of the Darkling Woods, desperately trying to remember everything that Arthur had taught him about tracking prey. All around him the trees were alive with the cries of unseen creatures, and the wind moved the treetops so that the air was filled with the constant hiss of rustling leaves.

Eventually she stopped, and Merlin crouched down

behind the trunk of a twisted oak, attempting to avoid the dead leaves and dry twigs that, to his ears, cracked like thunder every time he moved. Morgana had come to a halt in the centre of a small clearing, and was now pacing back and forth, agitated and nervous, obviously waiting for someone – or something.

She didn't have to wait long. With a low thrumming beat of hooves, three horses emerged from the darkness, pulling up sharply in front of her. One by one the hooded riders dismounted.

Merlin peered through the undergrowth. Two of the riders wore thick, ragged clothes and he could see a livid red emblem on their breastplates. It was the same tree motif that had been on the dagger they had found in the sentry. The Bloodguard.

Merlin's heart sank. Morgana was in league with them!

The third figure was smaller, more athletic. If Merlin had any lingering doubts that Morgana was the traitor within, they were banished when the figure pulled back her hood. His breath caught in his throat: it was Morgause.

He crept forward, straining to hear her words.

'I'm sorry you had to wait,' she said as she approached Morgana. 'There was much to discuss.'

'But your visit was successful?'

Morgause's reply chilled Merlin's blood. 'Cenred's army ride for Camelot on my command.'

Morgana smiled appreciatively. 'There is nothing you cannot do.'

'It is you who gives me strength, sister.' Morgause smiled at her. 'How goes the battle for Uther's mind?'

Merlin inched forward on his belly through the dead leaves. He had to get nearer to hear what they were saying clearly!

'When Cenred marches on Camelot he will find a kingdom without a leader,' said Morgana proudly.

Morgause pursed her lips. 'Then finally we are ready.'

'Not quite.'

Morgana turned and walked across the clearing. Merlin froze. She was coming right towards him. Had she seen him? He pressed himself flat on the ground.

'Merlin has guessed my intentions.'

Merlin tried to slow his panicked breathing. She knew of his suspicions . . .

'Has he told Arthur?' There was concern in Morgause's voice.

'Not yet.'

'Then we must stop him.'

'That will not be difficult.' Morgana sounded almost amused.

'Why?' Her sister was puzzled.

'Because he's already here.' Morgana turned her head, staring right into Merlin's eyes, her face a mask of cruel malevolence.

Merlin scrambled to his feet, backing away from her. Her lips curled in an unpleasant smile, her entire bearing was confident, supremely sure of her power.

'Do you really think I'm that stupid, Merlin?' she snarled.

Merlin didn't hesitate. He ran.

The Bloodguard drew their swords and raced after him, crashing through the undergrowth. Merlin didn't look back. He was younger and more agile than them – he was certain that he could lose them.

But he had not realized that Morgause was accompanied by more than two of the dark knights. A tall shape suddenly loomed out of the darkness in front of him. Merlin skidded, desperate to stop himself falling headlong.

A fist clad in chain mail crashed into his skull, and Merlin's world dissolved into pain and then silence.

Chapter Nine

Gaius knocked gently on the door of Arthur's chambers. There was no reply. He pushed open the door and entered quietly. The prince was standing at the window, staring out over the rooftops of the lower town, watching the smoke from dozens of fireplaces curl into the night sky.

'How are you?' Gaius asked gently.

'It's not me that's sick.' He sounded tired.

Gaius crossed to his side. 'It can't be easy to see your father this way.'

'No . . .' Arthur hesitated for a moment, then turned to the physician, his face anguished, his voice cracking. 'He's always been so strong. A warrior. A leader of men. He lifted this kingdom from its knees, Gaius . . . To see him now . . .'

The prince struggled to keep control of his

emotions, and suddenly Gaius could see so much of his father in him.

'I'm sure that, over time, he will recover,' he reassured him.

Arthur nodded sharply, his voice suddenly strong and certain again. 'I know that you will do what you can.'

'But until then, we have to make plans, Arthur.'

The prince eyed him cautiously. Gaius knew that there was no going back now. 'We need you to assume control.'

'That's ridiculous.' Arthur was quick to rubbish the suggestion.

'Camelot needs a leader,' urged the physician. 'It falls to you – you must fulfil your role as regent.'

Arthur shook his head, refusing to accept what Gaius was saying.

'This is not just me talking, members of the court have spoken—'

That was a mistake. Arthur turned on him, his face flushing with hurt and anger. 'So now you have taken to whispering behind my back. What kind of treason is this?'

Struggling with emotion was not the only thing that Arthur shared with his father, Gaius thought ruefully; he had inherited his temper too.

'It is for the good of the kingdom—'

'I am not going to usurp my father!' shouted Arthur.

'The palace is awash with rumour . . .' Gaius was determined to impress upon the prince the severity of the situation. 'The people are restless—'

'I don't give a damn about the people!' Arthur cut across him, shaking with fury. 'I swore allegiance to my king, and as long as there is breath in his body it is my duty to uphold that.'

'Arthur, please . . .' Gaius pleaded, but the boy's mind was made up.

'You are giving up on my father,' he said accusingly. 'That is something that I will never do.'

Merlin opened his eyes, wincing at the bright dawn light that filtered through the trees. For a moment he struggled to remember where he was, baffled as to why he was outside instead of tucked up in his bed; but as he tried to sit up, the sharp pain in his temples reminded him of exactly where he was and what had happened to him.

He was suddenly aware of something restraining him. A thin chain bound his arms and legs. It didn't look all that substantial. He tugged at it experimentally.

Noticing the movement, one of the Bloodguard came over to him and pulled him to his feet. Merlin's head swam and a wave of nausea swept over him. He was dragged across the clearing and dumped unceremoniously at the feet of Morgause. He could see no sign of Morgana.

The sorceress regarded him with amusement. 'You intrigue me, Merlin,' she murmured. 'Why does a lowly servant continue to risk everything for Arthur and for Camelot?'

Merlin said nothing, but she was watching his every move, his every expression. 'You know the answer, but you're not telling me – why?'

Merlin shrugged.

'Come on.' Morgause was becoming impatient. 'Time and time again you put your life on the line – there must be a reason.'

'I believe in a fair and just land,' Merlin told her defiantly.

She laughed. 'And you think that Arthur will give you that?'

'I know it.'

'And then what?' Morgause sneered at him. 'You think you'll be recognized, Merlin? Is that it? All this so one day you can be a serving boy to the king?'

Merlin stared silently at her, refusing to respond to her taunts. She must never discover the truth about the power he possessed. He had no way of knowing what she might do with that knowledge and he had no wish to find out.

The sorceress sensed his reluctance and crouched down, peering into his eyes. Merlin was suddenly struck by how beautiful she was.

'No,' she purred softly, her eyes boring into his. 'There's still something more. There's something you're not telling me, isn't there?'

Merlin shook his head, desperate to break away from her intense scrutiny. 'I've told you.'

But her patience was at an end. 'Well, you can take your secret to your grave.'

She rose, her eyes blazing with power as she intoned a spell.

'*Weorp untoworpenlic.*'

The chain that bound Merlin's arms and legs shimmered with an incandescent light.

'You chose to poison one of my own.' All softness had vanished from Morgause's voice now. 'You may regret that.'

She turned and swept out of the clearing, her Bloodguard in attendance. Merlin regarded the gleaming chain dubiously. Insubstantial it might have been, but he had little doubt that Morgause's enchantment had now made it unbreakable.

He allowed himself a little smile of triumph. Unbreakable for anyone who didn't know magic, perhaps – and thankfully his abilities were a secret that he had still managed to keep from her.

As Camelot came alive with the dawn, Gaius busied himself in the small kitchen in the corner of his chambers, heating a small pan of porridge. He ladled some into a couple of bowls and glanced over at the door to Merlin's room. Normally the smell of porridge was enough to rouse the boy from his bed. For such a scrawny thing he had a healthy appetite.

'Merlin,' he called.

There was no response. Gaius sighed. That boy really was his own worst enemy. If he was late yet again to attend the prince . . .

Gaius placed the steaming bowls down on the table and crossed to Merlin's room.

'Merlin . . .' He knocked loudly. Still no response. He pushed open the door. 'You're going to be late—'

The words dried on his lips. Merlin's bed was

empty, the covers still pulled up neatly. It hadn't been slept in.

Merlin had waited until he was certain that Morgause and the Bloodguard had gone and that he wasn't being watched, then turned his attention to the chain. If it had been fastened using magic, then it could be unfastened in the same way.

He centred his breathing, concentrating on the power that rested deep within him, bringing it to blazing life behind his eyes.

'*Abrecap benda.*'

He tugged at his bonds. There was no movement.

He uttered the words again:

'*Abrecap benda.*'

Still the slender chain held him fast. Frowning, Merlin tried another spell, summoning all his reserves of power.

'*Irenfaestnuga onlucap me!*'

He strained against the silver links, but if anything, the light from the enchanted chain blazed brighter. Merlin slumped back to the ground. Morgause was too powerful a sorceress, her magic too strong for him. As he sat there, regaining his strength, replenishing his power, a noise from the undergrowth made him start.

He looked around, but he could see nothing through the shadowy trees. A sudden horrible thought struck him: Morgause hadn't left him here on his own on a whim; she obviously had some plan for him. Some plan that involved him being stuck alone and helpless in the centre of the Darkling Wood.

As the noise from the undergrowth came again, Merlin started to get frightened.

Guinevere was replacing the flowers in Morgana's chambers when Gaius came hurrying in. Her smile of greeting faded when she saw the worried expression on his face.

'Have you seen Merlin?' he asked anxiously.

'Not since yesterday,' she answered, concerned by his demeanour.

Morgana entered the room behind him. Gwen quickly busied herself with her duties once more, not wanting to provoke her mistress's displeasure again.

'Is there a problem?' asked Morgana.

'I'm not sure,' said Gaius, frowning.

'What is it?'

'Merlin didn't come home last night.'

'That's not like him.'

'No.' Gaius turned and hurried from the room.

As he left, Gwen could swear that she saw a smile twitch at the corner or Morgana's lips. She shook her head. She was being unfair. Her mistress's uncharacteristic tetchiness earlier had her seeing things that weren't there. She knew that Morgana could never think ill of Merlin.

In the Darkling Woods the noises that Merlin had heard had become louder and more frequent, and now they came from all around him. Shadowy shapes flitted at the edge of his vision. He struggled to shut them out and focus on freeing himself, but he was now certain he knew the fate that Morgause had in mind for him.

He searched his memory for knowledge of spells of containment and entrapment, desperate to find an incantation that would counter the one that Morgause had used. As the clicking and droning grew closer, he took a deep breath and bellowed another arcane chant.

'*Min strangsst miht hate pe tosprigan!*'

As the spell died on his lips, there was a rustle in the undergrowth and a huge shape emerged stealthily into the clearing. It was a Serket, a giant scorpion-like creature with a deadly sting. The monster stopped, its segmented body glistening, its legs picking almost delicately at the leaves and mulch. Mandibles dripping with slime, it clacked its razor-sharp claws menacingly as its beady eyes fixed on the helpless Merlin. He stared in horror as the thick scorpion's tail arched high into the air, the wickedly sharp tip already starting to ooze with venom.

As he watched, more and more Serkets started to emerge from the wood. Merlin struggled futilely with the chains as the chittering horrors edged closer and closer.

Chapter Ten

Arthur sat at the king's bedside, staring down at the troubled, tormented face. He felt utterly helpless. His father had always been so powerful, so strong. Even when the two of them disagreed – and that was often – Arthur had always admired Uther's single-minded certainty. To see him like this, to know that his condition might well get worse . . .

The prince had never experienced such a feeling of hollow dread about the future.

He looked up as Morgana slipped into the room and joined him at Uther's bedside. For a moment they just sat there silently.

'I need him to get better,' Arthur said eventually.

'I know.' Morgana took his hand and squeezed it gently.

He turned to look at the girl with whom he had

shared so much of his childhood. 'I'm glad you're here,' he said quietly.

'So am I.' She smiled. 'I'll make sure he's looked after, don't worry.'

Underneath the king's bed, unseen by the prince, the mandrake root pulsed wetly, its black poison pooling thick and wet on the stone floor.

The Serkets were getting closer – dozens of them, all different sizes, their mouthparts moving hungrily, their claws clacking and snapping.

Merlin realized that his magic could be better used than in endless vain attempts to loose his bonds. He uttered a spell of banishment.

'*Awendap eft wasaelinga neatu!*'

Screeching horribly, the creatures scattered, retreating back into the safety of the trees. Merlin breathed a sigh of relief. It seemed to have worked – but before he even had a chance to feel pleased with himself, one of the larger Serkets pushed back through the undergrowth and edged slowly into the clearing once more.

One by one the others followed suit, more cautiously than before, but still hungry, predatory. Merlin's heart began to pound. The Serkets were bold, tenacious and vicious. They had some resistance to the banishment spell; he would have to try a different approach.

He reached within himself once more, his eyes flaring.

'*Mines bedbodes gemyndig, gap nu!*'

The skittering creatures stopped dead, pincers poised, rooted to the spot by the incantation.

Exhausted, Merlin closed his eyes. The effort of casting so many spells in such a short space of time was taking its toll, and his head was still pounding from the blow that Morgause's guard had dealt him.

The snap of a Serket's claw cut through the silence. Merlin opened his eyes in disbelief. Slowly the creatures were starting to come back to horrible clicking life, first one, then another and another . . .

'*Forlet me a!*' screamed Merlin, desperately snatching protection spells from his memory.

The monsters in front of him scattered in alarm, but he was suddenly aware of something moving in the shadows at the edge of his vision.

It was too late. A giant Serket burst out of the trees behind him. Before Merlin could roll out of the way, its tail scythed through the air, the razor barb stabbing into his shoulder.

The warlock screamed. The pain made him strong

and the power burst from him, lashing out at his attacker. It screeched angrily as it was hurled across the clearing, scattering its fellows as it tumbled through the air.

Merlin could barely breathe. The pain that surged through him was like nothing he had ever felt before; it burned through his veins like fire. Already he could feel numbness in his hands, and every breath was becoming harder and harder. Through blurring vision he could see the Serkets gathering for their final attack. Merlin knew that this time he would not be able to hold them back.

With consciousness slipping away from him, he threw back his head and started to speak in a strange guttural tongue, his voice deepening. The words boomed around the forest:

'*O drakon, e male so ftengometta tesd'hub'anankes.*'

For a moment the Serkets hesitated in their relentless advance, chittering agitatedly as the words echoed through the clearing.

Merlin drew in another ragged breath and, with his final ounce of strength, roared up into the sky:

'*Eukeo, nun entend'agag'emas ed fulaxon!*'

Then the pain overwhelmed him and he slipped into merciful oblivion.

★ ★ ★

On the Great Plains, a long line of soldiers marched in a dark swathe across the scrub; at their head, King Cenred himself led the way determinedly towards Camelot.

Morgause watched with amused satisfaction, the image of the huge army swirling through the faceted depths of her great crystal. She curled her hand and the scene swam closer. Cenred was mounted on a great black steed, the very picture of a courageous leader. But his jaw was clamped tight, his brow furrowed by the task he had set himself. Or rather, the task that Morgause had set him. She laughed. What a simple thing it was to control men such as this, to cloud their minds with desire, to tempt them with thoughts of power and wealth and adoration.

The sorceress waved her hand again, and the image of Cenred and his army faded from the crystal. If only Uther could have been controlled so easily, but he had closed his mind to the world of the magical, and that was a difficult barrier to breach. His son too was stubborn and strong-willed, but they both had a weakness – their love for Morgana – a weakness that she intended to exploit to its full advantage.

Soon word of Cenred's approach would reach the castle, and then panic would spread, people looking to their ruler for guidance, and finding that there was none to be had. By the time the army reached the castle walls it should be child's play to take Camelot; and then the time of Uther Pendragon would be at an end and magic would rise again.

Morgause felt a surge of excitement. To use magic openly again, to wield the power as was her right, to live like a civilized person, not skulking in a cave like some wild animal . . . Anger made her eyes flash in the firelight. She would enjoy taking her revenge upon those who had wronged her. Arthur, Merlin—

She stopped herself. Of course, Merlin would already be dead by now. She wished she could have stayed to watch his terror as the Serkets did their work. Perhaps she would return to the clearing when their task was done, to see if the creatures had left something for her – a keepsake to remind her of him.

She smiled grimly. Somehow she doubted that those monsters would leave anything at all.

Merlin was barely breathing when the first of the Serkets reached him. Hissing hungrily, the creature reached out with a serrated claw, tugging experimentally at his clothing. As if satisfied that its prey was no longer a danger, it reared up and gave a shriek of triumph.

A shadow suddenly spread over the clearing, and

a great wind started to buffet the trees. The Serkets scattered in panic as something vast and ancient descended from the sky, landing in the clearing with a force that shook the ground. Those Serkets that weren't crushed underfoot by the Great Dragon turned and scurried for the trees – but with a mighty bellowing roar, it breathed huge gouts of fire at them, sending them tumbling end over end, boiling them in their shells. The air was filled with the screams of dead and dying creatures, flames crackled through the undergrowth and acrid smoke billowed towards the darkening sky.

The Dragon turned and regarded the unconscious warlock at its feet. With a delicacy at odds with its size, it reached out with a claw and scooped up the limp body, cradling it almost tenderly to its chest.

With a single beat of its huge, leathery wings the Dragon launched itself into the air, sending the smoke swirling through the clearing.

When the smoke cleared, the Dragon was gone.

Chapter Eleven

The cave was immense, a vast cathedral carved out of the rock millions of years ago by a river long since gone. On a great pinnacle of granite a huge creature stood in silent vigil over the body of a young boy. Thin tendrils of smoke swirled around the boy's body, moving unlike any natural mist. For a long time the Dragon watched, unmoving, until, with a groan, the boy finally stirred.

Merlin woke to find the Great Dragon staring down at him, its huge, golden eyes regarding him carefully.

'I didn't think you'd answer my call,' said Merlin weakly.

'Merlin' – the Dragon's voice, rich and ancient, boomed around the cavern – 'I could not resist a Dragonlord – even if I wanted to.'

'I'm grateful. Thank you.' Merlin tried to rise, but

pain overwhelmed him and he slumped back, gasping with the effort.

'Lie still,' the Dragon insisted.

'My head . . .'

'The Serket's poison is powerful. I have given you an enchantment that will help you heal – but it will take time.'

Merlin had no strength to argue. He rested his head on the cool stone, and surrendered to sleep once more.

The morning sun rose over Camelot, making the castle gleam. A gentle breeze fluttered the pennants; the lower town was quiet and calm.

Inside Gaius' chambers, the atmosphere was anything but calm. Gaius was just sitting down to his breakfast when Arthur burst through the door. The old man looked up in alarm. The prince was only half dressed.

'Where is that half-wit?' bellowed Arthur.

'Merlin?' Gaius was puzzled.

'I've got no socks, no breeches and an archery session to go to.' Arthur stormed over to the door to Merlin's room. 'Merlin!' he yelled.

'I thought he was with you,' said Gaius.

'Don't try and cover for him,' snapped the prince.

'He didn't come home last night,' explained Gaius worriedly. 'I can't find him.'

Arthur shared none of Gaius' concerns. 'Well, when you do, you can tell him he's the target practice.'

The prince strode from the room, slamming the door behind him.

Frowning with concern, Gaius barely noticed him go. Where on earth had Merlin got to?

Morgana made her way towards Uther's chambers with no attempt at concealment. She had realized that subterfuge was no longer needed. She was the king's ward – it was only right that she should come to his chambers so often, understandably anxious about the welfare of her ailing guardian.

Careful to carry an expression of worried concern on her face, Morgana approached the guards who had been placed at the king's door. Bowing respectfully, they let her pass, moving a discreet distance away from the door to allow her some privacy.

As the door closed, Morgana's gentle expression changed, and she glared in revulsion at the man lying in the bed. She reached into her robe and removed the fresh mandrake root that she had hidden there. One eye on the door, she unwound a length of twine, looping it around the top of the dark, dripping root.

With a sharp tug she pulled the twine tight, wincing as the piercing shriek of the mandrake cut through the room. Uther's eyes snapped open, wild, terrified, darting to and fro. Morgana waved a hand in front of him but he paid her no heed. He could see nothing except the private horrors that inhabited his dreams and nightmares.

Morgana smiled and stooped to tuck the dripping mandrake beneath his bed.

Merlin woke with a start, roused from his sleep by a distant, piercing scream. Or so he had thought. Now that he was awake he could hear nothing. He sat up, realizing with surprise that the Great Dragon was still resting alongside him, waiting, watching over him as he slept.

'You shouldn't have let me sleep.'

'I had no choice, young warlock,' said the Dragon gently. 'The venom was too strong, even for your great powers.'

'I don't have time. I have to get back to Camelot.'

Merlin climbed unsteadily to his feet, wobbling precariously on the rock perch. 'The kingdom is in danger and it's my fault.'

He gazed up at the Dragon. 'I should have listened to you. I should never have trusted Morgana.'

'You did what you felt was right. And that shows great courage.' The Dragon studied him closely. 'But trust is a double-edged sword.'

'I thought because she had magic . . .' Merlin started to explain, then shook his head sadly. 'I thought we were the same.'

'In some ways you are.'

'No.' Merlin would not accept that he and Morgana were similar in any way. 'I will never be like her.'

'You have learned an important lesson, Merlin. Your kindness is your own worst enemy. Your determination to see goodness in people will be your undoing.'

The warlock said nothing. He knew that the Dragon was right: he had refused to take heed of the warnings he had been given, blinded to Morgana's true nature by the thought that she might be the one person with whom he could share his secret. More than anything he wanted someone to accept him for who he was; not to have to live in fear of revealing his gifts. That desire had clouded his judgement, his instincts. It had nearly killed him.

The Dragon seemed to sense his conflict. 'I cannot clearly see your fate, but I fear your futures are now joined for ever.'

'What do you mean?' asked Merlin. The Dragon had already revealed that his life was for ever linked to that of Arthur – but Morgana . . . ?

'She is the darkness to your light.' The Dragon looked sombre. 'The hatred to your love.'

Merlin thought long and hard for a moment, then turned away. 'I have to get back to Camelot.' He got up and took a few shaking steps.

'You're not fully recovered, Merlin,' insisted the Dragon. 'And it's more than three days' walk.'

Merlin turned back to the Dragon with a smile. 'I've no intention of walking.'

Merlin clung to the neck of the Great Dragon, the wind sweeping through his hair as the huge creature soared majestically through the moonlit sky. It was almost enough to banish the memory of the pain and fear and blackness of the last few days, and Merlin had to restrain himself from laughing out loud with delight.

As they cleared the tops of the Mountains of Isgard, the Dragon dived down through the clouds, and Camelot suddenly loomed out of the valley before them, proud and strong, its lights shining like a beacon in the night.

The Dragon circled the treetops, getting lower and

lower until it came to land in a clearing in the forest. The great beast dipped its head, allowing Merlin to slide down its neck and drop to the ground.

'This is as far as I go,' it growled.

'Thank you,' said Merlin gratefully. 'I won't forget this.'

The creature leaned close, fixing him with its icy glare. 'Be careful, young warlock. The great battle for Camelot has begun. You must be strong, for Arthur's destiny and the future of Albion lie in your hands.'

With that, it stretched out its wings and, flexing its muscles, lifted into the sky once more, hovering there for a moment, a vast, terrifying silhouette in front of the moon, before swooping away into the night.

Merlin watched it go. During their short time together the Dragon had been many things: mentor, friend, ally . . . and enemy. The only constant was that it always departed leaving him with more questions than answers. Merlin sighed. Friend or enemy, he would be dead without it . . .

Pulling his jacket tight against the night chill, the young warlock hurried towards the castle.

Gaius was sleeping soundly in his bunk when Merlin burst into the room and shook him awake.

The old man rolled over and stared blearily up at him, unsure whether he was real or part of a dream. 'Merlin?'

'You need to wake up.' The boy's voice was urgent. There was trouble. It was real enough.

'Where have you been?' spluttered Gaius, sitting up and rubbing his eyes.

'I don't have time to explain.'

Merlin handed Gaius his tunic. The old physician hauled himself out of bed and started struggling into it.

'Are you all right?' he asked indistinctly as he pulled the tunic over his head.

'Morgana is in league with Morgause,' explained Merlin. 'She's plotting against Uther.'

Gaius' head emerged from the neck of the tunic with a shocked expression on his face. 'What!'

Merlin looked at him in exasperation. He had his tunic on backwards.

'She's responsible for his visions!' Merlin hauled off Gaius' top, turned it round and pulled it down over his head again. 'Come on, hurry. There's something I need to show you.'

Struggling with his buttons, Gaius hurried after him.

★ ★ ★

As Merlin and Gaius approached the king's chambers, they could see that something was wrong. The two guards that Arthur had posted outside were standing in the corridor, peering in through the open door, their faces pale and frightened.

Gaius pushed past them. The room was dim – the only light came from the fire that blazed and spat in the hearth, but it was enough to see that the place was in complete disarray. Sheets had been thrown from the bed and strewn across the floor, furniture was overturned and smashed, tapestries torn from the wall. Of Uther there was no sign.

Gaius gestured to Merlin to move carefully, and the two of them edged nervously into the room. As they made their way forward, a pale shape became visible in the far corner. Gaius hurried forward.

'Uther,' he whispered, clearly shocked by what he had found.

The king sat on the stone floor, his eyes wide and staring, his jaw working silently as he stared at some invisible horror. He reached out with a trembling hand and grabbed hold of Gaius' arm, helpless with fear.

Merlin's heart sank. He was too late. The king had lost his mind.

Chapter Twelve

Uther was barely aware of the people around him; all he could see was the figure by the window, the figure that had come to his quarters, that had reached out for him, accusing, condemning . . .

He peered with trepidation through the gloom. The figure was still there, deathly pale – a warrior, his robes tattered and worn, his armour tarnished and dented. Blood trickled thickly down the dead skin of his cheek and, though the fire blazed, icy vapour poured from the warrior's mouth, cold, reeking of the grave.

It was Gorlois. Morgana's father. Dead Gorlois.

Uther felt the screams welling up inside him.

As Gaius struggled to free himself from the king's terrified grip, Merlin dived under the bed, groping for the mandrake root. He squirmed with revulsion as his fingers closed on the slimy knot of fibre. He tore it free, scrambling out from beneath the bed and tossing the vile lump into the roaring hearth.

A high-pitched scream tore through his brain as the flames engulfed the root. He clamped his hands over his ears but the noise was inside his head, deafening, inescapable. Thick sap boiled and spat as the flames caught hold and, with a horrible sizzling, the root shrivelled into nothingness.

As it turned to ash, so the noise abated in Merlin's head. The king too regained some control and, with Gaius' help, hauled himself to his feet.

'It was Gorlois,' he exclaimed weakly.

'Gorlois is dead,' said Gaius firmly. 'It was an enchantment, sire.'

'I could feel his breath – it was icy cold—'

'Sire!'

The urgent tone made Uther stop. He turned to his physician, his face pale. 'It was him, Gaius.'

The old man refused to be drawn into yet another argument with his king. 'You need to rest . . .'

'He was here . . .' insisted Uther, but didn't resist as Gaius led him back to his bed.

He sat down heavily as the physician took a small bottle from his pouch and emptied it into a goblet.

'Please, drink this . . .'

Uther stared at the goblet blankly.

'It will help you sleep.'

Reluctantly the king lifted the sleeping draught to his lips.

Back in the quiet of his chambers, Gaius was angry and concerned by what he had learned.

'The mandrake root is cruel, Merlin,' he muttered, pacing around the heavy oak table. 'It plays on the victim's darkest fears. The scars it has left will not heal quickly.'

Merlin nodded. 'We must tell Uther what Morgana has done.'

Gaius stared at him in disbelief. 'Are you mad? He would have our heads if we made such accusations – he would see it as treason.'

Merlin's face fell. 'But we can't just let her get away with it!'

Gaius sighed. For all his power, sometimes the young warlock could be monumentally naïve. 'Merlin, he dotes on her every word . . .'

'But if he knew . . . ?'

'You've seen how blind he is to her faults . . .' The old man stopped his pacing and sat, thinking.

'Besides, the root has gone now. It can do no more harm.'

'You don't understand,' Merlin insisted. 'I heard Morgana and Morgause – there is more to their plan, I'm sure of it!'

Gaius stared at the boy whom he had sworn to protect. Merlin had been through a lot over the past few days – the two sorceresses had been to a lot of trouble. Much as he hated to admit it, Merlin was right: it would be very surprising indeed if their troubles were over. Morgana would almost certainly try something new.

'Then we must remain on our guard,' he said gravely.

Dawn came over the kingdom of Camelot, but Sir Leon wished that the sun had never risen on the scene below. In the valley that formed Camelot's eastern border, a black line snaked to the horizon, a ribbon of men and horses. Swords and maces gleamed in the morning sun and Sir Leon could hear battle cries and the distant clank of armour.

It was as he had feared. It was an invasion: an invasion that had come because Camelot was weak and leaderless.

He looked at the faces of the knights alongside

him and saw something that he was unaccustomed to seeing. Fear.

In the fractal depths of her seeing-crystal, Morgause saw the concern on the knight's face and shivered with anticipation. Without their leader the Knights of Camelot were vulnerable, and without the knights, the kingdom would fall.

As the sun rose in the sky, Merlin entered Arthur's quarters and threw back the curtains. There was a cry from the bed as the sunlight flooded the room. He turned to greet the prince, and his face fell. The room was in a state of chaos: dirty plates piled on the tables, heaps of unwashed clothes on chairs and hanging from cupboards, pieces of armour, the metal dull and lifeless, discarded in every corner.

'What's happened?' he asked in shock.

'What's happened?' groaned Arthur, dragging himself from his bed. 'I've had to make do without a servant, that's what happened!'

Merlin couldn't believe it. 'I wasn't gone that long!'

'It was without my permission.' The stern tone left him in no doubt that the prince was annoyed with him.

'What if I was dying?' asked Merlin quickly, keen to defuse any potential argument.

'I wouldn't be complaining,' Arthur said, glaring at him. 'So where've you been?'

Merlin decided that honesty was the best policy. 'I was dying.'

It was the wrong decision.

'I don't have time for this, Merlin!' shouted Arthur. 'The future of the kingdom rests on my shoulders – do you have any idea what that feels like?'

Merlin found himself formulating a rather too truthful answer again. 'Well—' he started, but the prince cut him off.

'Merlin, I should throw you in the dungeons. What do you have to say for yourself?'

His servant decided to change the subject. 'You've not had your breakfast this morning, have you?' Food was always a good way of diverting the prince.

It didn't work.

'I'll have *you* for breakfast.' Arthur snatched up an empty goblet and hurled it at him.

Merlin ducked. 'Missed.'

A plate sailed after the goblet. He dodged that too. 'It's no wonder this place is in such a mess,' he chided.

As Arthur heaved a piece of his discarded armour

into his arms, Merlin decided that it was time he made himself scarce.

'I can see you've got all the makings of a great king,' he said, ducking out of the room as the armour crashed into the door frame.

Morgana rose late, a rare luxury for her. For as long as she could remember, mornings had always been difficult, a struggle to wake after a night plagued with nightmares and visions. All that had changed with Morgause.

Getting out of bed, she stretched lazily, luxuriating in the sensation, grateful that at last her life was set on the path that had long been so cruelly denied her.

She put on a robe and crossed to the breakfast table, picking at the meat and fruit that had been left for her. While she ate, she stared out at the morning sun as it warmed the white stone walls of the castle. As she did so, the door to her chamber opened and Guinevere slipped nervously into the room.

'May I clear away the dishes, my lady?'

Morgana was about to reply when she caught sight of something that brought all the demons from her past life back from her subconscious. Arthur was walking across the courtyard below her

window, and in his wake, wittering on incessantly
. . . Merlin.

She felt the panic well up inside her, threatening to
overwhelm her. If Merlin was here, alive . . . If he had
spoken to Arthur . . . If they were on their way to see
Uther—

'Morgana?'

Gwen had obviously sensed her distress. Morgana
tried to slow her racing pulse.

'I was thinking what to wear.' She turned from the
window and smiled weakly at her servant. 'I must
dress.'

Gwen nodded and hurried to the wardrobe to find
her mistress something suitable. Meanwhile Morgana's
mind was racing. How had Merlin escaped? More
importantly, what were his plans now that he had?

Later that morning, with the fact of Merlin's miraculous
escape still buzzing through her head, Morgana made
her way to her guardian's chambers to remove the spent
mandrake. A fresh one would need to be placed there
that evening, and Morgause had promised that all would
be ready for her.

As she slipped into the dim, curtained room and
crossed to the king's bed, she stopped for a moment,

frowning. Uther looked . . . peaceful. Surely the mandrake should have done its work?

As she bent to retrieve the root from beneath the bed, a low voice echoed from the gloom.

'Have you lost something, my lady?'

Morgana spun round, eyes narrowing as a figure rose from his seat against the far wall and made his way towards her.

Gaius. Morgana cursed him silently. The old man was cunning – almost as much of a danger as Merlin. She waved a hand airily.

'An earring . . . I thought I might have dropped it here yesterday.'

She turned to the sleeping king, hiding the anger she felt. 'How is he?'

'Much better, my lady.' Gaius' voice was without emotion. 'We found the source of the sickness. He was being enchanted.'

Morgana's heart raced at the words. Did they *know*?

'Enchanted?' she asked innocently, aware of the tension in her voice.

'You need not worry, he will make a full recovery.'

'That is a relief.' Morgana had to force the smile to her lips.

'Indeed, my lady . . .'

Gaius held her gaze for a moment, his ancient face unreadable; then, with a curt bow, he turned and left the room.

Morgana glared after him. It was all starting to go wrong!

Merlin hurried towards the throne room with some trepidation. Everyone had been summoned to hear Sir Leon's report about the army massing on their eastern borders. It was a full meeting of the Council.

Which meant that Morgana would be there.

Merlin wasn't sure what he would do when he saw her. More importantly, he wasn't sure what *she* might do.

When he arrived, the councillors were already seated at the long rectangular table, listening to Sir Leon. Uther was the notable absentee. The throne of Camelot was empty.

Merlin could feel Morgana's eyes boring into him as he took his seat next to Gaius. Her hatred was palpable.

Arthur stood at the window, listening as Sir Leon reported on the army that he had seen approaching.

'I estimate they will reach the city within two days,' he told the councillors.

Arthur's face was grim. 'Under whose banner do they march?'

'Cenred's, sire. We knew he was amassing an army—'

'How many men?' snapped Arthur impatiently.

Sir Leon took a deep breath. 'Twenty thousand men, maybe more.'

Merlin could see the shock on the prince's face. He glanced over at Gaius.

'I fear the news of the king's illness has spread beyond our borders.' The old physician's voice was grave. 'Cenred sees an opportunity.'

Sir Leon nodded. 'Then we must find a way to appease him.'

'That's not what my father would do.' Arthur's voice rang out strongly across the council chamber. 'He would not bow to our enemies.'

A murmur ran through the Council.

'Forgive me, sire,' ventured Gaius, 'but we are out-numbered two to one.'

'And what concessions will Cenred insist on? What territories will he demand?'

'We do not have to give him anything,' Gaius pointed out. 'But it could buy us valuable time.'

'It shows weakness, Gaius,' growled Arthur. Merlin

knew that tone of voice. The prince was not going to be argued with. 'How long before Odin sees an opportunity too? Or Caerleon? Or Alinor?'

The murmurings of the councillors faded as Arthur made his way up to the throne of Camelot. For a moment he hesitated on the steps, as if suddenly aware of what it meant to take his father's place. Merlin too felt a rush of exhilaration, a foretaste of the destiny that, if what the Great Dragon foretold was right, he and Arthur would one day share.

Arthur turned and sat down, staring hard at all those watching him. 'There is only one course of action open to us . . . We must prepare the city for siege.'

Chapter Thirteen

The tension in the council chamber erupted into a nervous chatter. To commit Camelot to a siege was a huge step. For such a decision to be taken by the prince and not the king . . . The concerns of the Council were voiced by Sir Leon.

'Are you sure that is wise?' he ventured.

'The castle is our strongest weapon,' said Arthur firmly. 'No army has ever taken Camelot.'

'But what about the people in the outlying villages?'

'We will give them refuge within the city walls.'

'And what of their houses, their livelihoods?' Sir Leon looked to the Council for support. 'Cenred will destroy everything in his path.'

'But they will have their lives.' The prince's voice hardened. 'Go! Ready the army!'

The councillors began to file slowly from the room.

Arthur sat on the throne, watching them. Was this what it was like every time his father made a decision? Seeing the eyes of those who disagreed with you, hearing the mutterings of dissent from those who considered their own plans better? He hung his head. If Cenred's army was as large as Sir Leon had estimated, then it was a long hard road that he had started down, for both himself and his people.

'Your father would be proud.'

Arthur looked up to find that Gaius had waited behind. The old man approached the throne.

'That cannot have been easy for you.'

The prince sighed, unsure whether it was proper to admit his doubts, even to such a trusted adviser as Gaius.

The physician seemed to sense Arthur's unease. 'Taking all matters into consideration, sire, I think your decision was a prudent one.'

Arthur relaxed. If Gaius agreed with him . . .

'Anything you want to talk about, anything you need . . .' Gaius smiled.

The prince felt a surge of gratitude that the man who had advised his father so wisely was prepared to extend the same wisdom to him.

'Thank you, Gaius.'

After the council meeting, councillors, knights and

court officials had gathered in concerned groups in the corridor outside. Merlin had used the throng to keep well clear of Morgana, waiting until Arthur emerged.

The prince strode past him down the corridor, his handsome features clouded with uncertainty. He looked so troubled that Merlin felt the need to offer some encouragement. He hurried after him.

'You did well in there.'

Arthur barely heard him. 'Hmm.'

'I mean it. I was impressed. You were much more . . .'

Arthur turned and stared at him, waiting.

Merlin flushed. 'I don't know . . . What's the word . . . ? Commanding?

'You tell me.'

'Well, normally you're not that authoritative . . .' Almost immediately Merlin knew he had said the wrong thing.

The prince stopped. 'I lead an army, Merlin.'

'Of course.' Merlin tried to backtrack. 'It's just . . . well . . . If you think about it, this is different – this is daunting.'

Arthur glared at him. 'Thanks.' He started walking again.

'It is,' insisted Merlin, running to catch up. 'We're

talking siege engines, battering rams, catapults . . . You made a tough decision. I mean, you're risking hundreds of people's lives. Men, women, children . . .'

Arthur stopped again. 'You know what?'

'What?'

'I'd really prefer it if you could just keep quiet in these situations.'

Merlin looked hurt. 'I was only trying to help.'

'Well, you're not.'

Merlin shook his head. 'I know you don't mean that. You're just worried. But you don't need to be. Look at what we've got . . .'

Arthur gazed around despairingly. 'What?'

'You and me!' Merlin grinned.

'Merlin, what exactly are *you* going to do?' the prince said in exasperation.

'I'm going to be at your side.' The young warlock had been buoyed up by the speech that Arthur had made in the throne room. 'Like I always am. Protecting you.'

Arthur rolled his eyes. 'God help me!'

'We won't let Camelot fall.' Merlin tried to sound convincing.

'That's reassuring, Merlin.' The prince shook his head wearily. 'If I need someone to make me feel terrible in the heat of battle, I'll just come to you. In the meantime . . .' He glared at his servant meaningfully.

'Your armour needs cleaning?'

Arthur nodded.

Merlin watched as he marched off down the corridor. He really didn't know what Arthur would do without him.

Later, as Merlin returned to the prince's quarters, laden with gleaming metal, he realized that Arthur's decision to barricade them all inside the castle had been taken without knowing all the facts. Would he be so keen to follow this course of action if he knew the identity of the traitor within the walls? If he knew about the alliance she had made? He mulled over how best to voice his concerns. Despite Gaius' warnings about what would happen if he made an accusation against Morgana, he was beginning to think that he had no choice.

He was so wrapped up in his quandary that he didn't notice the figure lurking in the shadows until it was too late. A slender hand reached out and hauled him into a doorway, fingers digging painfully into his arm.

Morgana.

She glared at him, her face inches from his, her eyes

blazing with anger. 'I don't know how you managed to escape,' she hissed. 'But I do know one thing – if you breathe a word of what you saw, I will make your life a short and painful one.'

Merlin pulled himself free, every sense alert, waiting to flee at the first sign that she might try to injure him.

But she merely smiled coldly. 'Just think how Uther would react if he learned how a serving boy had tried to poison his beloved ward.'

Then she pushed past him and vanished down the passageway. Merlin watched her go, despairing at the hatred that he had seen in her eyes. She was right. She didn't need to do anything to him. If she needed to, she could play the role of the poor, wronged ward to perfection and Uther would dispense his justice in a heartbeat.

Merlin shook his head. There was no point in trying to convince his master of what he knew. He was going to have to come up with something else.

Arthur sat by the window of his chambers, watching as his men started to make preparations for the coming battle. Supplies were being brought in from the lower town; grain stores and larders were now full to bursting with essential supplies. Fortifications were being strengthened and defences prepared at the gates and on the battlements.

Arthur ground his fist into the stone of the window-sill. Had he made the right choice? Was this the best way to deal with the army that was approaching their borders, or should he be leading his knights to meet them head on? He flushed, angry with himself: his father would have had no such doubts, of that he was sure. When Uther made a decision, it was with complete certainty, and the people obeyed without question.

The prince stared down at the crowd milling around below his window. How many of them thought that he had made the right decision? he wondered. How many would stand firm when their houses and farms were being burned by the approaching rabble, or when the first of them died from lack of food or water?

He just wished that he could be certain—

Gentle knocks on his door made him start, snatching him from his concerns.

'What?!' he snapped angrily, expecting to see Merlin's gormless features appear in the doorway.

To his surprise, it was Guinevere who stepped hesitantly into the room. Arthur stood up, immediately regretting his harsh tone.

'Guinevere . . .'

'I'm sorry' – Gwen hovered in the doorway – 'I didn't mean . . .'

'No, come in, please.' As always, Arthur was surprised by how easily the sight of Guinevere could lift his spirits, even in his darkest moments.

'How is your father?' she asked gently.

The prince sighed. 'I could do with him here.'

'You should have more faith in yourself.'

Arthur smiled gratefully at her; at least she believed that he was doing the right thing. 'What do the people say?' he asked.

'They're glad that you have taken charge.'

As answers went it was fairly non-committal. They might be glad that he had taken charge, but did they trust in his decisions? 'But I've committed them to a siege,' he blurted out, thankful for the chance to voice the concerns that he had been wrestling with. 'There are going to be casualties, Gwen.'

He turned back to the window. 'Perhaps Sir Leon was right. I should ride out to meet Cenred in open battle and save the townsfolk the horrors of war.'

Gwen shook her head. 'The likelihood is that you would lose. And then how long would the city stand?'

Arthur said nothing. Gwen was merely telling him things that he already knew.

She came across to his side. 'I trust you, Arthur. More than Uther, more than any man.'

He looked down at her, his heart swelling with gratitude and . . . something else. Something deeper. His skin tingled as Gwen placed a gentle hand on his shoulder.

'Worry is not a wise counsel. Forget everything else – you have to follow what you believe is right.'

He covered her hand with his own, feeling the warmth of her touch, the smoothness of her skin. They stood like that for what seemed like an eternity . . . then Gwen pulled her hand away abruptly, shooting a frightened glance towards the open door.

'I should go, sire.'

Arthur shook his head. 'There's no need to call me that.'

Gwen gazed into his eyes. There was so much that she wanted to say to him, so much that she knew she could never say. To see him so alone, so isolated . . . It was more than she could bear. She desperately wanted to put her arms around him, to give him the strength he needed; but now, more than ever, she needed to treat him as the prince, as the future king. 'There is every need, sire.'

They looked at each other gravely for a moment, then she turned and hurried from the room.

Alone once more, Arthur stood listening to the sounds of preparation ring around the castle courtyard, lost in his own concerns again.

By the time Morgana finally managed to escape the castle walls and make her way to the Darkling Woods, it was late and the moon was rising. Ever since she had caught sight of Merlin in the courtyard, she had been desperate to warn Morgause, but with the entire city preparing for the coming siege it had been all but impossible.

Arthur had wanted to post two guards at her side for her protection, and it had taken all her powers of persuasion to convince him otherwise. It was only when night had fallen and the curfew had come into effect that she had finally been able to slip from her room and make her way through the lower town. There had been soldiers everywhere, and finding a horse had been difficult. Soon it would be impossible to get out of the city without being seen.

Morgana waited for what seemed like an age amid the rustles and cries of the wood. Her only chance of getting back into Camelot was while it was still dark, and already she could sense the first fingers of dawn about to light the distant horizon. If she could not warn her sister . . .

Finally she caught the sound of distant hoof beats, and a figure on a pale horse came racing through the swaying trees. Morgause.

Morgana hurried forward as the sorceress slipped off her mount. 'Where have you been?'

Morgause frowned. 'What's wrong, sister?'

'It's Merlin . . . He's alive. He is back in Camelot.'

For a fraction of a second Morgause's icy composure almost crumbled, a flicker of concern creasing her pale brow.

'That is not all . . .' Morgana was desperate to unburden herself of all that had happened. 'He has thwarted us – he has destroyed the mandrake root – your enchantment has been broken.'

Morgause's mask of calm superiority slammed down once more. 'Do not worry. Cenred's army is less than a day from the city.'

Morgana had not realized that they were so close. 'Then it is time . . .' she murmured.

'Are you ready?' Her sister's eyes bored into her.

She nodded – but Morgause could sense the hesitation in her. 'Morgana,' she whispered, 'Cenred's army are mighty, but they cannot bring down the city on their own. You too must play your part.'

Morgana hardened her heart. She had come so far,

and this was not the time to show weakness. 'Tell me what I must do.'

The sorceress turned and untied a bundle from her saddle. She unwrapped the cloth to reveal an ornate staff, its wooden surface covered in runes and symbols. Morgana eyed it warily. She could sense the magical power within it – a force that electrified the air, intensifying the power that lay inside her.

Morgause caressed it tenderly. 'It was carved from the rowan tree that grows at the very heart of the Isle of the Blessed – only the high priestesses and their Bloodguard have ever set eyes on it.'

'My magic is still weak.' Morgana was not sure if she was ready for such power. 'I do not have the strength to wield such an instrument.'

Morgause just smiled. 'Don't worry. The staff will guide you – it carries its own power.'

Morgana tentatively took hold of it, feeling the complex and tactile carvings beneath her fingertips. 'I will not fail you,' she promised.

The sorceress's eyes flashed. 'I know.'

Chapter Fourteen

At dawn a steady stream of villagers made their way up from the lower town and across the drawbridge into the citadel of Camelot. Soldiers at the border had sent word that the approaching army was less than a day away, and Arthur had given the order that the people were to leave their homes and take shelter within the castle walls.

Gaius watched the hurrying hordes with sadness. When they returned to their town – *if* they returned to their town – then he very much doubted that there would be much of it left.

'Gaius . . .'

The old physician turned from the window to see Uther trying to raise himself from his bed. He hurried over to the king's side. Uther put a hand to his forehead and let out a low groan.

'The effects of the sleeping draught I gave you,' explained Gaius.

'I do nothing but sleep,' complained the king groggily.

'Hopefully things will start to improve.' Gaius felt his pulse, nodding sagely. 'I've found the source of your affliction.'

Uther watched him carefully, waiting for an explanation.

The physician hesitated for a moment. 'You were enchanted.'

The explosion of outrage that he was expecting did not come; instead Uther's eyes suddenly snapped towards the window in fright. Gaius followed his gaze to where the curtains had suddenly lifted in a breeze.

'I opened the window,' he said quietly.

'Close it,' Uther ordered, then lay back in bed, clearly exhausted.

Gaius crossed the room and shut the window. The enchantment might have gone, but the king was still reluctant to trust his own senses. That was not good for him – or for his kingdom.

'It will take some time for your mind to heal,' Gaius told him. 'But I promise you, sire, you will not be woken by any more apparitions.'

'No . . .' Uther's voice sounded drained. 'Only by my conscience.'

Gaius frowned. The king was strong, but even a strong man had his breaking point. He just hoped that they had put an end to the enchantment before it had done permanent damage. He decided that for better or worse it was time that the king knew the truth about his ailment.

'The magic used on you was powerful. We found a mandrake root beneath your bed.'

Uther was puzzled. 'How can this have happened?'

'I don't know, sire . . .' Gaius paused, aware of the reaction that his next words might elicit. 'I fear that we have a traitor in our midst . . .'

'A traitor with magic . . . ?' Uther's face darkened with anger.

'Indeed, sire.'

A loud cry from the courtyard distracted Uther once more. 'What was that?'

Gaius sighed. The truth was far preferable to any horror that the king might think lay beyond his walls. 'The castle is preparing for a siege.'

The news had a better effect than Gaius had hoped and seemed to galvanize Uther out of his lethargy. He threw off the bedclothes and struggled to rise.

'Fetch me my clothes,' he ordered.

'No, sire.' Gaius tried to stop him. 'You are still weak – Arthur has taken charge.'

'I am the king,' he insisted.

'I assure you he has everything under control.'

Uther struggled to free himself from Gaius' grasp but lack of food and days of sickness had taken their toll.

'You must listen to me,' the physician implored. 'It's not safe. You're not fit to fight.'

The king slumped back, breathing heavily, the exertion too much for him. Already his eyes were closing once more.

'You must rest,' said Gaius firmly.

The king had no strength left to argue. Within moments he had slipped into unconsciousness.

All through the castle everyone was making ready for the coming battle. In the dungeons, weapons were being removed from storage, soldiers forming a human chain to transfer spears and arrows to the knights on the battlements.

Arthur watched the preparations with satisfaction. Everyone was pulling their weight. Well, almost everyone. As he rounded a corner, he saw Merlin struggling with some heavy sacks.

'Merlin!' he bellowed. 'Where've you been? I've been calling you . . .'

The boy gestured proudly at the sacks. 'I've been gathering provisions.'

Arthur stared down at him in bemusement.

'Twenty-five salted cod, fifteen dried capons and' – Merlin patted a particularly bulky sack – 'one smoked boar.'

'What on earth for?' The prince couldn't believe his ears.

Merlin's face fell. 'We're preparing for a siege.'

'Yes, not a banquet!'

'You know what you're like without food,' Merlin reminded him. 'We could be trapped in here for weeks . . . months even . . .'

Arthur gave him a withering look.

'Look what I got for your breakfasts.' Merlin rummaged around in one of the sacks. 'Your favourite . . .'

He held up a jar. It contained some pale orbs bobbing about in a dark fluid.

The prince grimaced. 'Pigs' eyes?'

'Pickled eggs!' Merlin beamed at him.

Arthur sighed. The boy had no idea. 'I'd rather have pigs' eyes,' he muttered.

'I'll get some . . .' Merlin made to hurry off, but Arthur stopped him.

'No, we've got more important work to do.'

They made their way to the other side of the castle, where the passageways were being lined with beds, ready to accommodate the inevitable wounded. Womenfolk were preparing bandages, and hurrying from Gaius' chambers laden with potions and ointments.

Arthur joined Sir Leon to inspect the preparations, Merlin hovering in their wake. The prince caught sight of Gwen in one of the makeshift hospitals and the two shared a secret smile.

Aware that Merlin might have seen the moment of intimacy, Arthur turned and marched towards the courtyard, barking orders as he went.

'Has everyone from the outlying villages been given shelter?' he asked.

Sir Leon nodded. 'As best we can, sire. They amount to almost nine thousand so far, but they are still coming . . .'

Arthur nearly balked at the news, but kept his composure, aware that now, more than ever, he needed to hold his resolve. 'How long will our provisions last?'

'That depends, sire' – Sir Leon's voice was grave – 'on what losses we sustain.'

Arthur nodded grimly. 'And Cenred?'

'Our scouts report that he will be upon us in a matter of hours.'

In a wide clearing in the forest of Brechfa, on the eastern flank of Camelot, Morgause watched as Cenred approached with his guards. Behind her, impassive beneath their helmets, the men of the Bloodguard waited silently.

In her seeing-crystal the sorceress had watched as the army approached the border, and had ridden out to greet their leader, eager for the bloodshed to begin. Now it was upon them. All her plans, all her dreams, were just a few scant hours from completion.

Cenred smiled as he caught sight of her. He really was such a simple creature to control, she thought. A few whispered promises, a few simple gifts . . .

'My dear Morgause . . .' Cenred took her hand and kissed it, his eyes bright with anticipation.

'Cenred.'

'My army will be here by nightfall,' he announced.

Morgause couldn't help but smile. Cenred looked

like a puppy that had just done its master's bidding. 'I'm glad that pleases you,' he told her.

'I'll wait to see if you deliver before I say that I am pleased . . .' said Morgause coolly.

'And when I do . . . ?' Cenred sneered.

She extracted her hand from his grip. 'Then I will give you a feast that you will never forget.'

Arthur sat watching as his father slept. He had hoped that, with Gaius' discovery of the mandrake root, the king would recover swiftly, but it seemed that fate was not going to deal him that lucky card. Gaius insisted that Uther was no longer under any enchantment, that he would make a full recovery, but Arthur could tell that his continued malaise was as much a concern to the physician as it was to everyone else.

He sighed, wanting to say something to the sleeping figure but not sure what he *could* say.

He was suddenly aware of being watched and turned to find Merlin standing in the doorway.

'Sire? It is time.'

Arthur nodded and turned back to his father, suddenly finding the words he had sought: 'I promise that I will not let you down.'

★ ★ ★

As dusk fell, a single drum beat out a steady rhythm. On the battlements of Camelot Merlin stared out in shock at the army that had massed outside the castle. Row upon row of armoured figures glinted in the last rays of the dying sun; thousands of spears and swords gleamed; catapults and scaling ladders cast long shadows over the waiting soldiers, and the air was thick with the angry chants of the impatient invaders.

If Arthur was equally shocked by the size of the enemy that confronted him, he hid it well. Turning from his foe, he beckoned to Merlin to follow him to his chambers to prepare him for the fight.

The boy dressed his master with none of his usual banter. The single monotonous drumbeat resonated though the castle. It was obviously designed to unnerve them, but strangely Merlin found that it had the opposite effect; it gave him focus, allowed him to concentrate his thoughts.

Unfortunately his thoughts weren't on his duties. He fumbled with a buckle on the prince's breastplate. 'Sorry,' he muttered.

'Not like you to get nervous, is it, Merlin?' goaded Arthur.

'I'm not nervous,' he said simply.

'No?' The prince sounded doubtful.

'Because I believe in your destiny . . .'

Arthur snorted. 'Have you been on the cider, Merlin?'

Merlin found that the drumbeat had given him the words that he needed to say. Arthur had been his master, his ally and his friend. The Great Dragon had told him that their destinies would for ever be entwined, and somehow Merlin knew that however great the army was that massed outside their walls, this was not the hour of their defeat. Camelot would not fall to some rabble.

'It is your fate to be the greatest king Camelot has ever known. Your victory today will be remembered by every age, until the end of time.'

He handed Arthur his sword and scabbard. 'Just trust in yourself.'

The prince was taken aback, clearly moved by his servant's words. 'There are times, Merlin, when you display . . .' He shook his head. 'I don't know what it is. A sort of . . . I don't want to say—' he went on, floundering. 'It's not wisdom . . . But yes. That's what it is.'

Merlin smiled. To leave Arthur almost speechless was rare. To receive praise from him was rarer still. But his pride was short-lived.

'Don't look so pleased.' Arthur snatched the sword from him. 'The rest of the time you're a complete idiot.'

Morgana also listened to the sonorous drumbeat. Like Arthur, she was being dressed for the coming battle, but unlike Merlin, Gwen had serious misgivings about her decision.

'Are you sure about this, my lady?' she said as she tightened the straps on Morgana's breastplate. 'It's Arthur's job – the knights' job – to fight, not yours.'

Morgana looked at her disdainfully. 'If this last year has taught me anything, it is that we must all fight for what we believe is right.'

There was a curt knock on the door and Arthur entered the room. Gwen shot him an apologetic glance as she hurried out, leaving the two of them alone.

Morgana stared defiantly at the prince as he took in her armour.

'Morgana, your place is not on the battlefield,' he told her.

'And why not?' she snapped.

'I mean it.' Arthur's tone was dangerous. 'We spent too long searching for you to lose you again now.'

'You underestimate me, Arthur.' Morgana refused to be spoken to as if she were some runaway child. 'I am more than a match for any man.'

Arthur was all too aware of the truth of that. 'You are to stay inside the palace,' he insisted, smiling.

'Don't worry.' Morgana smiled sweetly back at him as he left. 'I have no intention of leaving its walls . . .' She was thinking of all the damage she could still cause from within . . .

The Knights of Camelot prepared silently for the coming fight. Each of them knew the enormity of the task that faced him; each knew that he faced an enemy with superior numbers and weaponry. But none shirked his duty. They were bound by oath to protect the kingdom and they would do so to their last breath.

They looked up expectantly as Arthur strode through their ranks. As he reached the door, he turned, his sword raised, his eyes shining with adrenaline at the battle to come.

'For the love of Camelot!' he roared.

The assembled knights raised their swords and voices in reply.

'For the love of Camelot!'

★ ★ ★

The drumbeat cut through the night air. As Morgause and Cenred watched, a group of mercenaries loaded one of the catapults with the first of its deadly cargoes. Abruptly the drum stopped. As it did so, a torch flared, and within moments the sky was filled with fireballs, arcing through the blackness and exploding in fury in the lower town.

Flames danced into the night sky.

The siege of Camelot had begun.

Chapter Fifteen

Uther twisted and turned in his sleep: his dreams were filled with the clash of steel on steel, the whinnying of frightened horses and the screams of the injured and dying.

His nose twitched as the smell of smoke caught at the back of his throat and he awoke coughing. The orange glow of distant flames lit up his chambers. This was no dream. His kingdom was under attack!

Uther struggled out of bed. As he got to his feet, his head swam – the floor seemed to be heaving beneath his feet. He steadied himself against the wall, slowing his breathing, trying to concentrate. He needed his armour, his sword . . . Slowly he made his way across the room to the stand where his armour was always laid out in readiness.

He dressed himself carefully and meticulously, the

ritual of donning his battle-scarred armour giving him strength. There was a familiarity about the routine that cut through his fatigue and hardened his resolve.

He was the king and his place was on the battlefield with his men.

Drawing his sword, he staggered out of the room, pushing his way along the bustling corridors and out into the courtyard.

The night air was filled with cries and curses; fireballs hurtled overhead, smashing into the city walls. Uther could see the scarlet capes of the Knights of Camelot as they fought a fierce battle in the lower town. As he struggled across the drawbridge, a figure emerged from the smoke and crowds, heading towards him.

Uther's eyes were streaming with tears – he couldn't tell if it was friend or foe. He raised his sword to defend himself; then, at the last moment, realized that it was Sir Leon, one of his own men.

The knight stared at him in astonishment. 'It's not safe. You need to go back, sire.'

Uther brushed him aside angrily and plunged on into the chaos.

Inside the castle the first casualties were starting to arrive. Merlin could see Morgana working alongside Gaius and

Gwen, bandaging wounds and helping to administer potions and ointments. To the casual observer she was the same kind-hearted girl that she had always been, but Merlin had no doubt that her true nature would soon show itself. The attack was the perfect time for her to slip away unnoticed.

He tried to catch the physician's eye. 'Gaius!' he hissed.

The old man looked up, and Merlin beckoned him over. 'One of us needs to keep an eye on her,' he said.

Gaius nodded. 'Don't worry, I am.'

'You mustn't let her out of your sight.'

There was a colossal explosion from outside as another fireball erupted into flames in the courtyard.

Merlin looked at his mentor. 'I need to get back to Arthur,' he told him.

With a final glance at Morgana, he hurried back out to find the prince.

He had barely left the building when a noise made him look up. A fireball was heading straight for him! He threw himself to one side as it smashed into the wall nearby, sending him tumbling across the cobbles. Flaming debris rained down around him. He glanced back to check that the hospital was still standing, but the walls of Camelot were strong and the fireball had done nothing more than scorch the stone.

Determinedly Merlin set off for the lower town.

On the hillside overlooking Camelot, Morgause sat astride her horse, watching in satisfaction as the flames started to billow into the night sky. She closed her eyes and breathed in deeply. She could smell the earthy tang of smoke and blood on the breeze. It would be a night that she would remember for a long time.

There was a blare of horns and she opened her eyes in time to see Cenred's men begin to storm the citadel. Huge siege ladders crashed against the white stone of the walls, and men swarmed up them. For a moment Morgause thought that the battle might be over even sooner than she had expected, but Uther's men were too well trained and valiantly fought off the attackers, sending them tumbling and screaming as they pushed the ladders back or sent down arrows in a deadly rain.

Morgause gave a hiss of disappointment. Compared to the Knights of Camelot, the army that Cenred had put together was an undisciplined rabble. Still, a rabble with sufficient numbers was still an effective, if unsubtle weapon. Camelot would fall eventually. It was just a matter of time.

★ ★ ★

Arthur and his men were engaged in fierce hand-to-hand combat with Cenred's forces in the lower town. The streets were littered with bodies, and fires blazed all around them as buildings and carts were set alight. A tangled barricade across the street was giving some advantage as it meant that Cenred's men could only come through in small numbers, and the Knights of Camelot were cutting them down in waves.

Arthur looked up as another knight rushed past him and joined in the fray. It was with disbelief that he realized it was the king.

He darted forward shouting, 'Father!' and grasped Uther by the arm, hauling him away from the oncoming mercenaries.

Uther shook himself free. 'What are you doing?' he asked.

'You're not well!'

'This is my kingdom,' bellowed the king.

Over his father's shoulder Arthur watched in despair as, on the other side of the barricade, his forces were overrun. Cenred's men surged forward in an angry tide.

'Pull back!' he cried. 'Retreat!'

The knights turned and ran for their own lines, aware that the battle for the lower town was lost. Sensing victory, the mercenaries unleashed a hail of arrows at them.

Knights crashed to the ground. Arthur looked on in horror as he realized that one of the fallen was his father.

He raced forward, kneeling at Uther's side. The king was twisting in agony on the ground, the shaft of an arrow protruding from his thigh. Arthur felt a surge of relief. As bad as the wound might be, at least his father was alive.

He grasped hold of Uther's arm, desperately trying to drag him to his feet, but his father bellowed in pain, his leg buckling under him.

Arthur half dragged, half carried him towards Camelot's lines, but Cenred's men were getting nearer to the barricade by the second.

They weren't going to make it.

Merlin arrived in the lower town just in time to see Arthur and his men retreat, and the arrow take down the king. Desperately he pushed through the tide of bodies that surged towards him.

The first of Cenred's men had reached the barricade and was levelling his crossbow at Arthur's back. Merlin reached out and felt angry fire rise behind his eyes.

'*Forbearnan!*'

The fires burning on either side of the barricade suddenly sent flames racing along the tangled timber to engulf the pursuing mercenaries. There were screams of agony as the street was suddenly blocked by a raging wall of heat.

Merlin hurried over to Arthur and caught hold of Uther's other arm. Together they carried the wounded king towards the citadel.

The makeshift hospital occupying the lower corridors of the castle was now overrun with the dead and dying – knights with wounds from close combat; villagers and servants caught in the lethal bombardment of fireballs. Gaius and his team of helpers were working flat out, but each time it seemed they were getting on top of things there was a cry from the doorway and another stretcher would appear.

Morgana was relying on another of those moments to make her move. She didn't have to wait long. A knight with a serious sword injury to his chest was rushed to a waiting bed. Gaius and Gwen hurried over to tend his wounds, and she saw her chance. As soon as the physician bent over to examine the new patient, she hurried for the exit and vanished into the crowd.

Gaius caught a flash of black at the corner of his vision and turned just in time to see Morgana dart out of the doorway. He cursed under his breath. The girl was cunning. He should have anticipated that she would do something like this.

Quickly he instructed Gwen on how to dress the knight's wound, ignoring her protests as he hurried out into the burning chaos.

The courtyard was a nightmare of flames and screams. He looked around in despair. How could he possibly find her in all this?

A sudden breeze made the acrid smoke swirl around, and as it cleared, Gaius suddenly caught sight of Morgana's slender figure on the far side of the courtyard. She seemed to be making for her chambers. Determined that she should not have the opportunity to put whatever plan she had into action, he hurried after her.

Morgana reached the sanctuary of her chambers without incident. People were too concerned with their own survival to take the slightest notice of her.

Quickly she hurried over to the cupboard where she had hidden the staff, and retrieved it, feeling the strange tingle as her fingers closed around the slender shaft.

As she made to leave, the sound of hurrying footsteps echoed down the corridor. Whoever it was was moving too stealthily to be a panicked courtier or frightened servant. She cursed. It could only be Gaius. He must have followed her.

Quickly she ducked behind a drape, pulling the staff close to her chest. She held her breath as the door edged open and Gaius slipped into the room.

The old man peered around the gloomy chambers, then turned and hurried away once more. Morgana took a deep breath, grateful that he hadn't thought to make a more thorough search.

She stepped out of her hiding place and scurried over to the door. The corridor beyond was empty. Clutching the staff to her chest, Morgana hastened to perform the task that Morgause had set her.

Uther grimaced as his son examined the arrow wound. The tip had come right through to the other side of his leg, and Arthur had already cut it off and removed the shaft. It was messy and painful, but not life-threatening. Uther had refused to take up a bed in the hospital or be removed to his quarters, insisting that they treated him on the steps of the great courtyard.

Now he was angry and impatient. Almost his old self, thought Merlin.

'You must get back to the battle,' he urged Arthur. 'We are losing the lower town.'

'It is already lost, Father.' The prince's voice was resigned.

Uther gritted his teeth. Arthur was right: there was no point in wasting more men and resources on a hopeless battle. They had to consolidate their forces.

'And the citadel?' he asked.

Arthur nodded reassuringly. 'Safe for now.'

'It must stay that way.'

The prince stopped attending to the leg wound and looked Uther in the eye. 'Father, you have to trust me. I know what I'm doing. You must rest. And when you are well again, you will still have a kingdom, I promise you that.'

The king regarded his son with pride. The boy had done well in the face of staggering opposition. But Uther knew him too well – he could see the strain in his eyes, hear the weariness in his voice.

The boy had done well, but was it enough?

Outside the citadel Cenred rode across to the hillside from where Morgause was observing the battle. She watched him climb the hill, grimacing with distaste when she saw the sweat and grime that coated his armour and skin.

'The lower town is ours,' he boasted proudly.

Morgause raised an eyebrow. 'That will hardly fill the pages of history. What of the citadel itself?'

Cenred's smile faded. He pointed at the castle below. 'Their defences are strong. It is time for you to deliver your side of the bargain.'

'Patience, Cenred.' Morgause tutted at him, as if he were an impatient child. 'You will not be disappointed.'

Morgana made her way down into the depths of the citadel. Soldiers and servants kept hurrying past her, desperate to deliver fresh weapons to the men on the front line. No one paid her the slightest heed. Clutching the staff, she pushed on, ever deeper.

Merlin helped Uther to limp into the makeshift hospital. Eventually loss of blood had forced the king to admit that he might need help, and with his son returned to the battle, he had been persuaded to visit Gaius. Townsfolk hurried forward to take care of their king, but of Gaius himself there was no sign.

Frowning, Merlin hurried over to Gwen. 'Where's Gaius?' he asked her.

Gwen looked up from the knight she was tending. 'I don't know.'

Worried, Merlin turned to go and find him. As he

did so, Gaius came in through the door. Merlin knew at once that something was wrong. The old man sighed wearily and gave him the bad news.

'Morgana has disappeared.'

In the ancient vaults deep beneath the citadel, Morgana stood and regarded the tombs of the long dead. It was exactly as she remembered from her childhood games: she and Arthur had once dared each other to touch the resting places of his ancestors.

Ranks of tombs lined the walls, their cracked and faded stone thick with dust and cobwebs. Torches guttered fitfully in alcoves in the walls, sending shadows dancing across the rock.

Morgana raised the staff high, then plunged it down, driving it through the solid rock.

At once it began to glow, illuminating the vault with an eerie light.

Merlin burst into Morgana's chambers, desperate to find her. As he did so, a tingling in his mind made him freeze. Something powerful – something old and dangerous and infinitely evil – was being used in the castle.

His heart sank. Whatever it was that Morgana had planned, it had started.

Chapter Sixteen

On the hillside overlooking Camelot, Morgause stiffened as she too felt the power of the staff. She let out a small sigh of satisfaction. Morgana had done well. There had been moments when she had begun to doubt that her half-sister had the courage to go through with the task she had been set. It seemed as if her fears were unfounded.

Cenred noticed her good mood. 'Enough of your games, Morgause,' he growled. 'What has happened to your traitor?'

Morgause sighed. 'For such a great king you have very little patience.'

'The time for patience is over,' he snapped.

'You need not worry much longer.' Morgause's voice was soothing. 'No army can fight on two fronts – not even the Knights of Camelot.'

Cenred looked at her in puzzlement. Morgause ignored him. She had an army of her own now.

In the vaults, the pale light from the staff grew in intensity, the air buzzing with energy. The light seemed . . . thick, alive somehow. It penetrated the cracks in the ancient tombs. Morgana stepped back in alarm as a sound like thunder rang out through the mausoleum and the lid of one of the tombs split open, as if struck by some great hammer. She watched in amazement as, one by one, the other tombs cracked apart, the noise deafening.

As the last echo died away and silence descended once more, she heard another sound – a click, a rattle, like dry twigs being tapped together.

A shadow suddenly lanced across the wall as something thrust its way out of one of the shattered tombs. It was a hand, but Morgana could see that this was no ordinary hand. The skeletal hand flexed experimentally. As she watched in horrified fascination, other hands emerged from the rest of the tombs, and the bodies of the dead started to crawl out of their resting places.

High above, a party of Cenred's men had finally succeeded in breaching the battlements, and now Arthur was leading a desperate battle to drive them back. The fighting was close and bloody, the stone walkways narrow and slick with blood.

Arthur parried a slashing blow and brought his elbow down hard on his assailant's unprotected neck. The man slumped forward and Arthur used the momentum of his falling body to heave him back over the battlements. There was an angry cry as the man crashed into his fellows below, and the prince allowed himself a small smile of satisfaction.

The smile faded as he saw one of his own men – one of the youngest of the Knights of Camelot – struggling to fend off the attack of an ogre of a mercenary wielding a vicious-looking mace.

Arthur hurried to assist but it was too late: the young knight's sword shattered under a crushing blow from the mace and he crumpled to the ground, his arm clearly broken.

The brute raised the mace again, but the prince lunged forward, running his sword through the man's chest and dropping him where he stood.

Arthur hauled the wounded boy to his feet and dragged him down the stairs towards the safety of the keep.

He came upon a group of women huddling together

in the cloisters. Arthur lowered the knight into their arms. 'Take this man to the hospital,' he ordered them.

He turned, ready to rejoin the battle, when he noticed a familiar figure emerge from a doorway into the courtyard.

'Merlin!' shouted Arthur. 'Where the hell have you been?'

Merlin looked as though he was about to tell him something, but then thought better of it. 'Nowhere,' he muttered.

Arthur didn't have time for games. 'You're making a bit of a habit of this. What's your excuse this time?'

The boy said nothing. His eyes were wide and staring, his jaw dropping open in astonishment.

'Come on, Merlin.' Arthur wasn't about to fall for that old trick. 'You can do better than that.'

Merlin continued to stare in horrified amazement. He raised a trembling hand, and pointed. With a prickling on the back of his neck, Arthur turned. And froze.

Three skeletons were emerging from the doorway to the vault, their yellowing bones cracking and grinding with every step. Each held a rusted sword.

Rotten teeth gnashing, the skeletons charged. Arthur barely had time to raise his sword before the first was upon him, slashing at him with its sword. He warded off the blow but the creature was fast, stabbing at him again and again, driving him back across the square.

Recovering his balance, Arthur dodged out of the way of the slicing blade and drove his sword into the creature's chest. Fragments of bone chipped and shattered, but the figure kept on coming. The prince backed away in alarm.

He glanced over to where Merlin was battling with another of the skeleton warriors, stabbing at it with a spear. He too was finding that his blade passed straight through the creature without the slightest effect. Obviously terrified, Merlin began to swing around blindly. A wild blow caught the skeleton on the shoulder, cutting off its arm.

The creature stopped, looking down at the empty socket for a moment, then launched itself forward once more, swinging its broadsword without the slightest concern for its missing limb.

Merlin dived out of the way, crashing hard onto the flagstones. The creature lurched past him, pursuing terrified townsfolk across the square. The boy lay winded, then suddenly sat up as a scratching, clattering noise caught his attention.

To his horror, the skeleton's arm started to claw its way across the ground towards him, fingers scrabbling as it hauled itself forward. Finding a discarded sword, Merlin slashed out at it desperately, but the arm kept coming, unstoppable, relentless.

Arthur raced over, kicking out at the arm and sending it clattering across the square. He hauled Merlin to his feet, dragging him through a doorway. The two leaned against the cool stone of the wall, catching their breath.

'You need to warn Gaius,' Arthur gasped. 'Tell him to seal off the hospital.'

They looked up in alarm as, with a clatter of dry bones, two more of the skeleton warriors appeared at the far end of the corridor. Arthur hefted his sword. Merlin tried to drag him away but he shook himself free angrily.

'Merlin, do as I told you!'

With a despairing look at his master, Merlin ran.

Sir Leon and his men were finally starting to hold off the advancing army. They had decided to make their stand at the drawbridge, where the narrow approach and steep sides of the moat were providing an effective barrier to the attacking hordes.

Sir Leon had positioned his men in a defensive wall, rotating archers and swordsmen in a well-rehearsed pattern. The Knights of Camelot were well-trained, used to taking orders and to working as a unit. Their opponents were undisciplined and impulsive, their attacks without order or plan. Already the road leading to the drawbridge was piled high with bodies and Sir Leon was starting to see fear in the eyes of the survivors. A few more unsuccessful attacks and their morale would fail.

He cried out, rallying his men. Camelot would not fall.

Suddenly a terrified scream rang out across the battlefield. Sir Leon frowned. The cry had not come from his enemies; it had come from behind him. He turned and stared open-mouthed at the skeletons that had emerged from the keep and were cutting a swathe through his men.

For a moment he almost faltered, but then rage made him strong. Their enemies must be desperate to use sorcery against the Knights of Camelot. They would regret it.

He gripped his sword tightly. 'On me!' he cried, and stepped forward to confront his new opponents.

Gaius was beginning to wish that Uther had not been persuaded to come to the hospital after all; he really was the most difficult and argumentative of patients. The physician had already had to redress the wound in his leg several times because of the king's refusal to stay still.

'I need to get out of here!' complained Uther for what seemed like the hundredth time.

'No, sire,' said Gaius patiently. 'You are still weak from the medicine I gave you – I told you this.'

'I cannot watch my kingdom fall and do nothing.'

'Arthur will defend it.' Gaius was firm.

He looked up as Merlin burst into the room and hurried over to him, grateful for the distraction. As the boy drew near, he could see the fear on his face and, with a chill, realized that things must have taken a turn for the worse.

'You need to seal off the hospital.' Merlin kept his voice low. 'The castle is under attack from within.'

Gaius was aghast. 'What are you talking about?'

'Morgana,' said Merlin bluntly. 'She's summoned an army of the dead. They're everywhere.'

The old man sighed. If only he had been able to stop her leaving. If only he had watched her closely as he had promised. He watched in alarm as Merlin snatched up a sword discarded by one of the injured knights.

'Where are you going?'

Merlin's face was grim. 'To try and stop her.'

★ ★ ★

The skeletons had overrun the castle. They kept emerging from the vaults like a plague of rats, the clacking of their bones ringing out along the corridors.

Arthur was exhausted. They were like no enemy he had ever fought before. The only way of stopping them was to hack them into separate pieces, and even then the arms and legs continued to thrash around like landed fish, grasping and hacking at anything that came within reach.

One of the creatures had entered the palace and had been making its way towards the hospital; Arthur had lured it aside and was now fighting a desperate battle to contain it. He felt his heel connect with the stairs to the upper levels and started to lead it upwards, exaggerating his tiredness to lull the creature into thinking he was beaten.

As they neared the top of the stairs, Arthur suddenly kicked out with a booted foot, sending the skeleton hurtling backwards. It crashed down the stairwell, limbs detaching as it went, shattering into a dozen pieces as it smashed onto the floor below.

Arthur slumped back on the stairs, struggling to catch his breath. He was suddenly aware of movement behind him, and looked up to see another skeleton towering over him, sword raised.

Chapter Seventeen

Merlin hared down the ancient stairs, taking them two at a time, barely able to keep his balance with the heavy sword in his hand. The steps were slick with water and the air cold and dank. Far below he could see the glow of an unearthly magical light; but more than that, he could feel the power that Morgana had harnessed, ancient and evil.

He reached the bottom of the stairs and stepped tentatively into the vault. Morgana stood with her back to him, a glowing staff beside her, throbbing with power. All around lay slabs of rock from the shattered tombs, leaving no doubt as to where the deadly skeleton army had come from. Morgana and Morgause had turned Arthur's ancestors against Camelot.

Sensing his presence, Morgana turned, her eyes

blazing with hatred and wild excitement. 'You should leave now, while you still can,' she snarled.

Merlin shook his head sadly. 'Stop this, Morgana, please. I beg you . . . Women and children are dying. The city will fall.'

'Good.' Her smile was vicious. 'Let Camelot fall – and those who rule it.'

Merlin couldn't believe there was nothing left of the girl whom he had befriended when he first came to Camelot. 'You don't mean that.'

'I have magic, Merlin,' Morgana told him, gesturing to the staff. 'Uther hates me and everyone like me. Why should I feel differently about him?'

'He loves you, Morgana. He's cared for you since you were a child.'

'He means nothing to me.' Her voice was cold, unemotional.

Merlin took a step towards her. 'You, of all people, could change Uther's mind . . . But doing this, using magic like this, will only harden his heart.'

For a moment there was the flicker of something behind Morgana's eyes, but in an instant it was gone. 'You don't have magic, Merlin – how could you hope to understand?'

'Believe me, I do understand . . .' Merlin faltered,

desperate to divulge the secret that had been a burden since he was a child, desperate to find someone who truly understood what it meant to have such gifts; but knowing that, if what the Great Dragon had told him was true, revealing his secret to Morgause or Morgana would bring nothing but misfortune and misery to all those he loved.

'If I had your gifts,' he said earnestly, 'I would harness them for good. *That's* what magic should be for. *That's* why you were born with these powers.'

The strength of emotion in Morgana's response took him by surprise.

'You don't know what it's like to be an outsider,' she cried in anguish. 'To feel ashamed of how you were born . . . To have to hide who you are . . . You think I deserve to be executed because of who I am?'

Merlin thought back to his first day in Camelot. To the execution in the square, to the glance he and Morgana had exchanged as they witnessed the unjustness of Uther's vendetta.

'No,' he said quietly.

'Merlin' – Morgana's voice was seductive, imploring – 'I want a kingdom where people are free to be who they are. Where I don't have to live in fear.'

As much as Merlin wanted to agree with her, he

could not bring himself to condone the path that she had chosen. Not at this cost.

'But you're destroying Camelot. People are dying at your hand . . .' he pleaded with her.

'Not as many as have died at Uther's . . .'

Merlin shook his head. That wasn't a good enough argument. 'Morgana, please . . . It doesn't have to be like this. We can find another way,' he insisted.

Morgana realized that her words were having no effect. 'There is no other way.' She turned away from him in disgust.

Merlin saw his opportunity and lunged for the staff, but Morgana was too quick for him. In a swift, sweeping movement she drew her sword, smashing the hilt into Merlin's stomach. He crashed to the ground, gasping for breath.

Morgana stepped over him, pressing the tip of her sword against his chest.

Merlin looked up at her sadly. 'What are you going to do – kill me?'

'You don't think I can?' she mocked.

He closed his eyes. The Morgana he knew was truly dead, and this monster had taken her place. 'If you're going to do it – make it quick.'

There was a rush of air as Morgana swept the sword

high into the air to deliver the killing blow. As she lunged forward, Merlin threw himself at her legs, sending her toppling backwards. He snatched up his own sword, but Morgana was already scrambling to her feet, her weapon ready.

Anger blazed in her eyes, and Merlin realized sadly that this would only end when one of them was dead.

Arthur rolled out of the way as the skeleton's sword sliced down. It was too late. The tip pierced the top of his arm and he cried out in agony. He rolled to one side as the creature turned to attack once more, kicking out at it as he had done with its fellow.

This time luck was not on his side and the skeleton easily avoided the clumsy attack. Aware that he could not win this fight with only one good arm, Arthur turned and fled. He had to get to the hospital and take his father to safety.

On the drawbridge, Sir Leon was managing to repel the advance of the skeleton warriors, but his men were now trying to hold off two sets of attackers at once. With their opponents distracted, Cenred's men were slowly making headway, forcing the Knights of Camelot towards the skeletons.

They were trapped.

The sound of steel on steel rang out through the vaults. Merlin had learned much about swordplay from Arthur over the years, but Morgana had known Arthur that much longer. The young warlock was able to parry and defend, but the upper hand was all Morgana's.

As Merlin began to weaken, she pressed home her advantage. With a swift flick of her wrist she sent his sword spiralling out of his hands and clattering into the shadows. Defenceless, Merlin waited for her attack.

Arthur staggered into the chaos of the hospital, just one of dozens of casualties of the skeletons' relentless attack. Gwen hurried him over to a chair and started to tend to his arm. In the background Arthur could see his father sitting silently amongst the injured, a broken man, his kingdom falling apart around him, his people dying.

The prince turned to Gaius, keeping his voice low so that his father would not hear. 'We cannot fight a battle on two fronts,' he said.

The clacking hollow sound of a skeleton and the scream of a soldier made him start. Gwen held him firmly as she tried to apply the dressing.

'Keep still!' she ordered.

Arthur grimaced as she applied a thick ointment to his arm. 'I don't know how much longer we can hold the citadel,' he said grimly. 'We need to get my father to safety.'

'How?' Gaius looked worried. 'We no longer control the lower town. There is no escape, Arthur.'

The sounds of battle grew still closer.

Arthur got to his feet and headed out of the hospital. Gaius might be right, but the prince of Camelot was not going to die without a sword in his hand, and his enemies – earthly or otherwise – would not take him without a fight.

As Morgana lunged at Merlin, sword outstretched, he skipped to one side, dodging the thrust and sending her off balance. Cursing, she stumbled, but before she could recover herself Merlin reached out a hand towards the vaulted ceiling, feeling the power blaze behind his eyes as he concentrated on the stone blocks above them.

'*Feoll bu brand . . .*'

The ancient stone crumbled and fractured, fist-sized lumps tumbling from the ceiling. One of them caught Morgana on the back of the head and she collapsed in an ungainly heap.

Merlin spun round, snatching up his sword and stretching his hand towards the glowing staff.

'*Snides* . . .' He muttered the magic word as he swung his sword.

There was a sharp *crack* as the blade sliced cleanly through the carved wood; as the two halves clattered to the stone floor, the eerie glow faded.

It was as if a puppeteer had let go of a string. All across the castle, the skeletons stopped in their tracks, their swords dropping from their hands, their bodies crumbling.

Arthur stared in astonishment as the creature he was fighting collapsed into a pile of dusty bones. He gripped his sword tightly. For whatever reason, the enchantment was over. Now he could concentrate on driving back an enemy that could be killed with a sword.

Rallying his men, the prince raced for the draw-bridge.

With the skeleton army gone, Sir Leon and his knights had already turned their full attention back to Cenred's mercenaries. The arrival of Arthur and his men added vigour to their defence, and within moments the attacking force had turned tail and was fleeing for the forest.

★ ★ ★

Cenred looked down in disgust as his men were driven from the lower town. He turned to Morgause angrily.

'Your traitor has failed us just as I knew they would. I'm calling off the siege,' he told her.

Morgause stared at him in horror, her mind still reeling from the destruction of her staff. 'You can't!'

Cenred glared at her. 'I cannot take the city unaided. That was not our bargain.'

He pulled on his reins and urged his horse down the path to rejoin his men.

'You've failed me, Cenred,' Morgause called after him.

'I would rather fail you, Morgause, than watch thousands of men die,' he replied.

The sorceress watched as he vanished into the drifting smoke. The siege of Camelot had failed. Her plan had come to nothing. It was over.

Chapter Eighteen

Dawn rose over a Camelot that was bowed but unbroken. Most of the lower town lay in ruins, the smouldering fires still casting a thick pall of smoke over the area. The white walls of Camelot were blackened and scorched from the impact of Cenred's fireballs, but from the towers the flag of Pendragon flew high and proud.

The people had suffered, but they would survive; the king had been sick, but he had recovered; and Arthur had proved to be the prince that the kingdom deserved.

In the throne room Uther had called a meeting to address the full Council, and as the courtiers gathered, Merlin hurried over to Arthur's side. During the night he had done a lot of thinking about what Morgana had said to him; about the lengths to which she was prepared to go. In the end he had decided that whatever the consequences, Arthur had to know the truth. He had to tell the king before he made his address.

'Sire . . .'

Arthur glanced down at him, irritated. 'What is it, Merlin?' he muttered.

Merlin took a deep breath. 'I need to tell you something about Morgana.'

'It's all right.' The prince turned his attention back to where his father was preparing to speak. 'We know what happened.'

'You do?' Merlin couldn't believe it. After all his agonizing, could it be that Arthur and his father had already realized who the traitor was?

Puzzled, Merlin wandered over to where Gwen and Gaius were standing.

If Uther and Arthur knew of Morgana's treachery, then why was she standing in her usual place at the king's side? As Merlin watched, Arthur took his place alongside her, and Uther turned to his gathered subjects with a grateful smile.

'In my time, we've won many battles, but none as important as this one,' he said, holding his arms out wide. 'Every man, woman and child played their heroic part – I thank and salute you all.'

A cheer rang out through the throne room; Uther raised his hands to quieten his courtiers.

'Before the battle, we knew we had a traitor in our midst; this traitor was nearly the undoing of us,' he told them. The hall was silent now, hanging on his every word. 'However, we have to give thanks to the one person who outwitted them, and almost single-handedly turned the battle.'

Merlin's breath caught in his throat. Surely no one had realized that it had been him . . . ?

'The Lady Morgana.'

Merlin couldn't believe his ears. Surely the man could not be so *stupid* . . . ?

'For it was she who bravely entered the vaults,' continued Uther, 'found the magical vessel and destroyed it.'

Merlin stared at Gaius in disbelief. After everything they had been through, after everything she had done, Morgana would go unpunished. Worse still, she was never even suspected.

'It only goes to show that now more than ever we must stand firm against the dark forces of magic. We must ensure that they never penetrate our walls again,' the king finished.

He turned and took Morgana's hand as the cheers

swelled once more. Merlin left the room in a daze. He had hoped – he had been certain – that the part Morgana had played would be found out. Now he had an enemy in the castle. He had thought that Uther was the only person he had to be wary of. Now he was in more danger than ever.

In the Darkling Wood, Morgause was waiting for her sister. Her plan had failed, but then, relying on others was always risky. Cenred had been weak, and was less in thrall to her than she might have hoped, and Morgana . . . Well, Morgause would have to wait and see.

A cloaked figure hurried through the trees and the sorceress moved to meet her.

Morgana's face was creased with worry. 'I'm sorry,' she stammered.

Morgause caught her hands. 'It's not your fault, sister.'

'But we have missed our moment.'

'Be patient,' said Morgause soothingly. 'Our time will come again, Morgana.'

'But what do we do now?' Morgana was desperate. 'What do I do?'

Morgause pursed her lips. 'Does anyone suspect you?' she asked.

'Just Merlin.'

The sorceress nodded. 'If he values his head, he will keep his mouth shut.'

'And if he does not?'

'Then I will deal with him,' said Morgause sharply. 'But for now you must play your part at court.'

'Please' – Morgana was almost in tears – 'do not make me go back there . . .'

Morgause shook her head sadly. 'I'm sorry, sister. But we have no choice. You must encourage Uther's love,' she told Morgana, 'for in the end it will prove a far mightier weapon than Cenred's army could ever be.'

Morgana bowed her head in despair. Morgause just smiled. Only time would tell if her sister had the strength to do what was required of her.

Merlin sat in Gaius' quarters, staring blankly at the huge wooden table. The old man set a bowl of soup in front of him and sat down.

Merlin looked up at him. 'Why is Uther blind to her true nature?' he asked.

Gaius shrugged. 'I don't know, Merlin. It is a mystery.' He paused. 'But Morgana will try again.'

'And I will be ready for her,' said the young warlock firmly.

'You must be careful.'

'I'm not afraid of her, Gaius,' Merlin insisted.

'You should be.' Gaius regarded him carefully. The boy had been through a lot, but he needed to control his emotions.

Merlin gave a deep sigh. 'All I feel for her is . . . sad. She's become so bitter, so full of hate.'

'Don't let that happen to you, Merlin,' Gaius said gently.

The boy shook his head. 'Nothing could ever make me that angry.' He picked up his spoon and took a mouthful of soup. As he did so, a voice rang out from the corridor.

'Merlin!'

The door slammed open and Arthur stormed into the room, his face red with anger. 'Get your lazy backside out here . . .'

Merlin looked at Gaius and frowned.

'On second thoughts . . .' Putting his spoon down, he hurried out after the prince.

Gaius just smiled and started to eat his soup.

ALSO AVAILABLE

THE NIGHTMARE BEGINS

When fire erupts in her chamber,
Morgana fears that she started the blaze
herself – using magic.

Frightened by this new power, Morgana
seeks out the Druids who Merlin believes
can help her. But Uther, believing she has
been abducted, sends an army after her.

Can Merlin find Morgana before
innocent lives are lost?

978 0 553 82204 5

ALSO AVAILABLE

THE LAST DRAGONLORD

A deep enchantment falls on Camelot
sending all its people to sleep, but why is
the Lady Morgana unaffected?

As the Knights of Medhir attack the
defenceless citadel Merlin must ask the
Great Dragon for help. But can Merlin
bring himself to pay the high price
demanded for Camelot's salvation?

978 0 553 82219 9